RUTHLESS
REIGN

ALEATHA ROMIG

NEW YORK TIMES BESTSELLING AUTHOR

Book #1 of the Royal Reflections series

Aleatha Romig

New York Times, Wall Street Journal, and USA Today
bestselling author

COPYRIGHT AND LICENSE INFORMATION

Ruthless Reign

Gowns, castles, and crowns make for the perfect reflections. Yet life isn't always as it appears. Illusions can distort visions, shadows still lurk in the sunshine, and monsters tread behind smiles and chivalrous facades.

Fairy tale dreams can turn into nightmares.

The world seems upside down to Princess Lucille when the man she loathes, her husband, Prince Roman, changes before her eyes. No one else appears to notice the nuances of difference.

Has the prince transformed?

Were Lucille's pleas answered?

Or has life as a royal become too much, transporting Lucille through the looking glass...where life is only a reflection?

From New York Times bestselling author Aleatha Romig comes a brand-new contemporary romantic-suspense series, Royal Reflections, set in the world of the royal elite, where things are not as they appear.

Have you been Aleatha'd?

*RUTHLESS REIGN is book one of the Royal Reflection series. This story continues in RESILIENT REIGN.

AUTHOR
NOTE

You are about to begin *Royal Reflections*. If this is your first meeting with the princess, prince, and Oliver, please begin at chapter 1. If you have read "Riled Reign," the prequel novella, you may jump ahead to chapter 8.

Either way, thank you for reading, and I hope you enjoy this unconventional royal romance...*The Crown* meets *Game of Thrones*.

~Aleatha

CHAPTER 1

Lucille

"Your Highness, it's nearly time," Lady Mary Buckingham said, opening the door and slipping into my private study aboard the royal jet. London, our next stop, was the third on our current Eurasia tour.

With nothing more than my mistress's address, my heart rate spiked, my mouth dried, and my hands became clammy. It wasn't Lady Buckingham who incited the visceral response; it was what her announcement signified. The plane was about to land, and in less than an hour, I'd be paraded around London on the arm of my husband, Roman Godfrey, the Duke of Monovia and crown prince of Molave.

To think that at one time, I'd been honored to be in the royal family's favor. Naively, I'd believed the fairy tales of princes and princesses. As the daughter of a baroness and an American politician, I wasn't unaccustomed to the finer things in life. I'd grown up in the lap of luxury in a three-story mansion within a building of mansions on the northern end of Midtown Manhattan, our windows overlooking Central Park. I attended the best private schools in the city and graduated with honors from Columbia University. My plans for my future included the work my mother loved—that of her charities and philanthropic events. I imagined helping others through my own efforts.

While I'd always been open to leaving the East Coast, I never dreamed of moving away from my native country.

Molave was a sovereign city-state on the southern shore of Norway. While my husband's country was relatively small in landmass, it was incredibly rich in natural resources—iron ore, copper, lead, zinc, titanium, and rhodium to name a few. Over the past few centuries, generations of the Godfreys have ruled Molave and benefited from its assets.

I first met Roman Godfrey at one of my mother's philanthropic events. High atop the New York City skyline in a swanky rooftop bar, our encounter resembled a choreographed movie. With the lights of the city as the backdrop, our gazes met from across the room. Conversations around us dimmed as the lights faded. Tall and handsome, Roman stole my breath and left me stirred in a way I couldn't describe. His dark gaze swept over me as if my designer gown was invisible.

His deep timbre and unique accent were sparks on flint. His rich cologne clouded my judgment.

In his presence flames ignited within me.

By the time Roman possessively took my cheek in his grasp, bringing my lips to his, there was an outright blaze. As we kissed, there was much I didn't know about him, including his title, and yet as I tasted the whiskey on his lips, I was intrigued.

When he asked to see me again, I agreed.

Little did I know that the meeting had actually been choreographed—arranged by my father and King Theodore of Molave, Roman's father. Without my input, a deal had been brokered. The king and a politician predetermined that I had the qualities compatible with the future king's only unmet need—a wife. I fit the bill: well-bred, well-educated, my own family wealth, and what some considered to be beauty.

Being that Roman Godfrey was nearing his fortieth birthday, he needed to wed.

Molave was also in need of allies within the United States. A congressman and heiress were the answer.

During Roman's and my whirlwind courtship, I was too infatuated with the man whose eyes I could become lost in to heed the warning bells. Covering the clapper in lamb's wool, I chose to keep those bells from ringing.

Roman's intensity for life should have frightened

me. Instead, it invigorated me. Soaring through the air in his two-seater sailplane created a rush unlike any other. His frequent disappearances came with explainable excuses. His ability to disappear while in plain sight sent chills through me that I learned to ignore.

When I voiced my concerns, I was reassured that marriage and family would help the prince overcome his anxiety.

Roman's quickness to anger should have been a waving red flag. Of course, at that time I equated his mood swings with difficult dealings regarding affairs of state.

With King Theodore aging, more and more was being expected of his son.

That exploding rage that reddened his neck and cheeks was never directed at me...until it was.

By then it was too late.

The entire world knew that an American woman from a prominent family was to marry the crown prince of Molave, one of the richest and most eligible bachelors in the world. While I'd read stories where the prince saved the day, I gravitated toward the stories where the woman, be she a princess or a commoner, saved the kingdom. That tale wove my desires to carry on my mother's work with my new title.

Not one of those fairy tales prepared me for what it would mean to marry a royal.

Marrying royalty was work—literal toil.

Six months before our wedding, I was whisked to Molave to begin the training and education I needed to hold a title. Weeks and months were spent studying Molavian history, politics, and economics. At the end of each day, I'd find myself in the king's study, reciting what I'd learned to either him or one of his top advisors. While I heard rumors about the king's demeanor, those months of training showed me a softer side of the monarch. Everyone had the same goal: to make me the best princess, duchess, wife, and ambassador for Roman Godfrey and Molave.

Despite talk of the king's failing health, five years later he was still in control.

Of course, during my indoctrination, there were also the lessons in etiquette with particular emphasis on royal traditions, as well as hours of work with a Lady Buckingham, my appointed Mistress of the Robes.

When another person was responsible for your every care, whether personally or by matter of oversight, there were no secrets. Despite the fact that Mary Buckingham was ten years my senior, after five years of marriage to the prince, I would consider Lady Buckingham to be my closest confidant.

"Your Highness," she said again, closing the door behind her. "We must prepare for the landing."

The hot tea I'd sipped in lieu of breakfast percolated in my stomach as I inhaled and stood. "You have my schedule." It wasn't a question. My daily activities came through her.

Lady Buckingham nodded, placing the printed schedule on the table before hurrying into the attached bedchamber and returning with my dressing gown. "I was just informed that there will be people at the airport. They've all been screened by His Majesty's Royal Service. Of course, you're to smile and accept their gifts."

Holding the dressing gown over her arm, Mary turned to me, and her gray eyes sparked with concern. "Princess Lucille, did you eat?"

As she spoke, I lifted the soft long shirt over my head and stepped out of the soft pants.

I'd objected to the idea of anyone besides my husband seeing me undressed. As I stood before Lady Buckingham in nothing more than my bra and bloomers, being intimately cared for was only one of the many concessions I'd made. Answering her question, I replied, "No. I'll eat later."

"Were you not brought your cooked breakfast?"

"I sent it away."

Her lips came together as her expression saddened. "I'll call for a cucumber and butter sandwich. While I know you're not trying, you are becoming increasingly thin. The royal physician said that it's important to have nutrients should you find yourself with child."

With child.

There was part of me who yearned for the days when people spoke in common phrases. Instead of with child, we would say pregnant—should I find myself pregnant.

For the record, I hadn't.

Countless physicians, surgeons, and specialists said I could and should.

I hadn't.

Once my morning resting clothes were removed, Lady Buckingham offered me the dressing gown. Sliding my hands into the sleeves, she proceeded to close the front and tie the sash.

As I sat, my mistress combed and styled my long dark hair. Next, she concentrated on my makeup. Once she was satisfied, she went back to the bedroom and returned with a lovely light-blue dress and jacket.

I stood and removed the dressing gown.

When she had the long, concealed zipper on the dress undone, Lady Buckingham crouched down and held the garment as I stepped into the circle. Soon, she had it pulled over my bra and bloomers. I slipped my arms through the sleeve holes. The sleeveless shift hung from my shoulders.

"It's supposed to be thirty degrees today," I said,

conscious of referring to Celsius versus Fahrenheit, as I eyed the matching jacket with three-quarter-length sleeves. "I'm afraid the jacket will be too warm."

As if I didn't speak, Lady Buckingham zipped the back of my dress and reached for my left wrist. She didn't need to verbalize her thoughts as she looked down at the now-greenish discoloration on my upper arm. Experience told me that the bruise would fully fade in another week to ten days.

"It would be best if you kept the jacket on during all the activities," she said.

Slipping my feet into the matching high-heeled shoes, I asked, "Have you seen the prince today?"

I hadn't seen him since we retired to the aircraft last night. The royal plane had separate suites for each of us, the same as our home, Annabella Castle, in Monovia.

Lady Buckingham shook her head. "From what I've heard, he's been working."

My breath caught. "What you heard?"

Had he been boisterous this early in the morning?

What would have set him off?

She nodded. "Lord Avery mentioned it."

I inhaled and lifted my chin. "I think I'd like that sandwich."

Lady Buckingham's smile returned. "I'll be only a minute. We must still add your jewelry."

My jewelry.

It wasn't mine. It belonged to the crown. I was only the model used to display the Molavian wealth. Whenever a jeweled bauble was placed around my neck, I had images of headless displays in a jewelry store.

Relishing the last few minutes of solitude, I paced the length of the small study as the jet descended, and beyond the windows, the terrain became more metropolitan.

"Three more cities," I told myself as a printed schedule caught my attention. While there were joint items on our schedules, it appeared that after the runway appearance and a joint meeting with our British counterparts, Roman would go one direction and I another. That was until we were required to appear together this evening at the banquet at Windsor Castle.

My eyes closed as I recited my pep talk.

Never had I imagined being an actor.

It was what I'd become.

And it was about time for the curtain to rise.

CHAPTER 2

Oliver

My thirteen-hundred-square-foot condo sat along a street lined with palm trees. Beyond my living-room windows, the Hollywood sign was visible in the distance. The Hollywood Walk of Fame was nearby as was the TCL Chinese theater, still referred to as Grauman's Chinese Theater. I was in the heart of Hollywood.

After a substantial stint on stage, my agent contacted me about the offer of a role as one of the lead characters in a popular futuristic comic franchise. The franchise approached me. My agent, Andrew Briggs—not related to the actor of the same name—proclaimed my ship had come in. The studio had a long list of sequels and prequels. Hell, there were even to be spin-offs.

Gold.

That's what he said.

Imagine my surprise when reading the revisions to the script for the upcoming release and I learned of my demise. My character would go out a hero, his reputation to be forever esteemed. Unfortunately, for me, that standing didn't come with prospects of future earnings.

"Sorry about dropping in before noon," Andrew said. "I have an afternoon flight out of LAX. Are you done filming?"

It wasn't unusual for him to stop by. However, it was usually on better terms.

"Yes, wrapped last night unless there are any pickup shots." I stared at my agent. "You weren't warned?"

Andrew shook his head as he walked back and forth in my kitchen. As he took a seat at the island, he said, "It's why I wanted to see you before I left town. I was caught off guard by your text."

"I was too shocked to call."

He grinned. "There's always voice work."

"Voice work?"

"You know, the franchise is looking at animation. *Clone Wars* has been a huge success."

With my hands flat and fingers splayed on the quartz breakfast bar, I took a deep breath.

"Your accents are fabulous," Andrew added. "There's no limit to what you're capable of doing."

While I was born in America, during my young, impressionable years, my mother was in the Air Force. Her career took my siblings and me to many corners of the world. When you're fluent in various languages, accents come naturally.

My dark eyes met Andrew's blue gaze. "You were the one who convinced me to leave New York. You said this series would be ongoing."

Not a bad-looking man, Andrew was a few inches shorter than I with the exact opposite coloring. As he sat and I remained standing, his complexion looked a bit off.

"Oliver," he said, "since you told me, I've been working on a few leads."

I'd already given this thought. Of course I had. Ever since reading the script that was like a gut punch to my stomach, I'd thought of little else. "I'm going to make calls to a few friends still on Broadway."

Andrew nodded. "A short return. I like it." He lifted his hands in a dramatic gesture. "Oliver Honeswell's Broadway return. It will be promoted as a limited engagement." He grinned. "I'm seeing the possibility."

Turning, I took in the view beyond the power lines of the city's rooftops and the Hollywood Hills. My mind filled with the rigorous schedule and rehearsals that came with live theater. Up until four years ago, I'd loved every minute. I was invigorated as the curtain rose, as the theater filled with patrons, as I became lost in the story we portrayed. The applause of a live audience was a drug. Ask any actor. It's addicting in the same way as alcohol or other drugs of choice. Each hit created hunger for more.

"What have you heard? Why did they kill me?" It was the question I'd not yet vocalized. Oh, I'd asked it in my head a million and one times. I'd contemplated the possibilities.

Andrew's sigh caused me to turn back as he ran his finger around the rim of the mug of coffee I'd offered.

"What did you find out?" I asked, uncertain if I wanted the answer.

He lifted his hand. "Rumor. It's all I have been able to learn."

"What rumor?"

He shrugged. "It was about the conflict."

Conflict.

My jaw clenched. "Rita? This is about me breaking off my relationship with Rita?"

"She" —he took a deep breath— "said she wouldn't continue filming if you were there."

"That's bullshit." My voice was louder than I intended. "Rita and I still talk. She was upset with the decision."

"What can I say?" Andrew said. "She's a good actor. Ronald didn't want to lose her."

"Fuck." Instead, they canned me.

Going to the liquor cabinet, I poured a shot of

whiskey into my coffee, lifted the rim to my lips, and took a healthy swallow. Raising the bottle, I wordlessly offered Andrew the liquor.

My agent shook his head. He'd stopped drinking alcohol years ago. Good to know the recent news of my demise wouldn't knock him off the wagon.

Taking another drink, my thoughts filled with the woman whom I'd dated on and off for a decade. Shaking my head, I muttered, "That bitch."

"You know she's been seeing Ronald?"

"Been seeing?" I asked, puzzled because she and I only split two weeks ago.

Andrew nodded. "For at least six months."

The whiskey in my stomach churned. "How did I not know?"

"You can understand how Ronald felt."

My eyes widened. "Ronald, the franchise producer?" The pieces of the puzzle were falling into place.

Andrew nodded.

That information put this in a whole new light. "The decision wasn't Rita's. It was fucking Ronald's. That whiny-ass piece of shit didn't want me around. I could break that sorry excuse of a man in half."

"Oliver, none of this is official. It's gossip. It's hearsay. However, it makes the most sense. Your character was revered and had his own share of fan base." He shrugged. "Rita's is bigger."

Rita Smalls and I had been an on-and-off item since before I moved to L.A. We met nearly fifteen years ago when we were both struggling acting students at the University of Chicago. The tabloids made it sound as if my part in the franchise was due to her influence. She opened the door, but damn it, I was the one who played the part, the warlord with a soft spot for the superhero played by Rita Smalls.

"Maybe it would be good for me to get out of this city for a bit," I mused. "I'll make that call to Ricardo and see if Broadway is a possibility."

"Do you still have it in you to perform on stage?"

I looked down at myself and back up. "Are you saying I'm out of shape?"

"No. Not at all. It's been a few years since you've belted out songs or danced your way across a stage."

"Only because warlords don't sing and dance. I'll do whatever I need to do."

Andrew pulled out his phone. "The Broadway thing is a great idea." He showed me the screen. "I'll send you Dustin's number, Dustin Hargraves."

"The voice coach? You think I need a coach?"

"I think it's been a bit since you've stretched your strengths." He smiled. "Not physically. Hell no. You've kept up on your training. I'd say being a warlord has made you even fitter than when you first came to Hollywood."

"Send me his contact information," I acquiesced.

"In the meantime, I have a few leads on commercial work."

I shook my head. "No go."

"There's a script I read recently for a sitcom. You know, they're coming back, complete with laugh tracks."

"Fuck that. I'd rather starve."

Pushing back the chair, Andrew stood. "I'm sorry, Oliver. I believe in you. You probably shouldn't have pulled out your dick where you work."

Shaking my head, I grimaced. "My dick never came out at work. Hell, I've known Rita longer than Ronald has." My whiskey-ladened coffee left a sour taste in my mouth at the thought of my dick being where Ronald's had been.

I needed to call my doctor.

"That may be true," Andrew said, pulling me from my thoughts of possible venereal diseases. "Despite being a whiny piece of shit, Ronald Estes holds power in Hollywood, especially at the studio. He promised Rita stardom beyond her imagination. It sucks, but you were the carnage left in the wake."

Sucks.

I scoffed. "Someone was sucked, and it wasn't me." I looked Andrew in the eye. "I'm not carnage. I'm not done acting. Fucking Ronald Estes can fire me from the franchise, but he sure as hell doesn't hold that much power over all opportunities. I'm not giving up."

Andrew nodded before finishing his coffee. "I'll be in touch. Let me know what Ricardo says, and give Dustin a call. He can help you brush up on your uncanny vocal ability."

After walking Andrew to the door and saying our so-longs, I waited until he should have made his way down the stairs to the street before I let out a roar. "Fuck."

My first instinct was to call Rita, but if Andrew was right, that conversation wouldn't do me any good. It probably would do me more harm. Pouring another shot of whiskey into what remained of my coffee, I went into the living room, sat on the couch, and turned on the giant television.

As I was about to change the channel, I caught a glimpse of the live footage. The prince and princess of Wales were hosting the crown prince and princess of Molave. The two couples were standing on a balcony, dressed in formal evening wear, smiling and waving at the crowd cheering them from below.

"Fucking ridiculous," I muttered. "You'd think this kind of shit would have been over centuries ago." Yes, I was speaking aloud to the television. "Maybe I should try a British or Molavian accent."

Wallowing in your sorrows could cause a person to speak to inanimate objects.

In retrospect, the television was a lousy conversationalist.

My head turned as the camera zoomed in on Princess Lucille. The sapphire-and-diamond choker around her slender neck glittered in the sunlight. "You're an American," I said to her beautiful smile and stunning blue gaze. "Fairy tales aren't real, at least for most of us." I lifted my mug in salute. "Good for you, Your Royal Highness."

That would be the life. Live in a castle. Let the taxpayers pay for your trips and...well, everything.

No wonder the different monarchies around the globe were facing backlash. The ceremonial shit on the screen was costing working people millions of dollars, pounds, rubles, whatever.

Turning the station to a rerun of a recent Lakers game, I muted the volume and called Ricardo. He answered on the second ring.

"Hello, warlord."

Yeah, the public hadn't been told the news of my demise. As far as I was concerned, the movie was a wrap. It still wouldn't release for another eight months. "Hey, I've been missing my roots. What's happening these days on Broadway?"

CHAPTER 3

Lucille

Silence loomed as Roman and I rode in the royal limousine back to the royal plane. Despite the late hour, the streets of London beyond the windows were alive, traffic bustling on the roads and people hustling on the sidewalks. Beside me, Roman sat statuesque, handsome as ever, dressed in his Royal Air Force uniform, complete with medals and ribbons. He wore a version of this uniform in our wedding. During my indoctrination, I learned all the ranks and titles he held.

Throughout the evening, I'd watched and listened. According to the news apps and reports I'd seen before dinner, there were discussions during the day between my husband, his British counterpart, and members of the British Parliament. Not all the reports were favorable to Molave, or more specifically to Roman.

Our tour was supposed to be a sign of good faith, of willingness to back our neighboring countries as tensions around the globe increased. While I'd been busy with tea, visiting a children's hospital, and a tour of Buckingham Palace, Roman had been tending to matters of state.

Even though my husband didn't share his concerns with me, I saw the stress in his eyes, the lines near their corners, and the rigidness of his jaw. My bachelor's degree was in political science. My lessons regarding Molave didn't end once we took our vows, and yet I was relegated to photo opportunities and discussions about my attire.

My dress for this evening's dinner was a floor-length ivory gown designed by Giorgio Armani. Lady Buckingham joked that it was in poor taste to wear the same designer as the hostess, in this case the princess. While I was a fan of Alexander McQueen, one of her favorite designers, this particular off-the-shoulder design nicely covered the bruise on my upper arm, making a jacket unnecessary.

I lifted my fingers to the sapphire-and-diamond choker around my neck as I imagined it tightening.

"Everyone speaks of your beauty," Roman said, breaking the silence and bringing my thoughts back to the present.

My hand dropped to my lap. With only the illumination from beyond the car windows, I bowed my chin once before responding. "I'm but the moon to your sun, Your Highness."

Roman hummed before reaching for my hand.

My skin prickled at the coolness of his touch as he lifted my knuckles to his lips.

The heat Roman used to conjure had dwindled to nothing more than a flicker of an extinguishing candle. I remained still, waiting for him to release my hand.

There were subjects that were off-limits with my husband; however, at this rare moment of affection, I chose to broach one of the subjects. "Are you well?"

Roman's dark stare narrowed. "Don't question my ability."

"I'm not. I'm concerned. There was a moment or two this evening..." I wanted to say there were moments when Roman seemed off, disconnected. I stopped as his grip of my hand intensified. Swallowing, I feigned a grin. "A moment or two this evening," I said again, adding, "when I longed to reach out to you."

"And that concerns you about my wellness?"

Tilting my head to the side, I replied, "I wondered if you felt the same way."

"You're my wife, my duchess, my princess. One day, you'll be my queen. You are mine to hold when I desire."

Nodding, I acquiesced, leaving my hand in his grasp as I turned toward the window and took steady breaths, hoping that whatever episodes I'd witnessed earlier wouldn't translate into a shared night with the man at my side. There was a pattern emerging, corre-lating times when his detractors criticized and critiqued with his dominating behavior with me.

Two more cities, I reminded myself.

"You know it," Roman said, his tenor deep.

I turned back. "It?"

"That many speak of your beauty." Releasing my hand, he ran his thumb over my cheek. "They say that I'm a lucky man."

The scent of liquor on his breath overpowered his cologne.

My pulse increased. "No, Your Highness, it is I who am lucky."

His lips curled into a grin. "As long as you under-stand your duty to me, to Molave."

"I do. I'm willing to do more."

Roman shook his head as his chiseled jaw clenched. "Do not start, Lucille."

With my chest tightening, I turned to meet his dark gaze. My knowledge and abilities were wasted as nothing more than an adornment. Taking a breath, I said, "More will not take away from my duties as duchess or princess. More would not change my duty as your wife. I want to help our people."

"*Our* people?"

"Yes, the citizens of Molave." With my marriage, I gained dual citizenship. "I've recently learned of some disparity in healthcare, not simply funding but in obtaining it. There was also a headline about concerns regarding imports. The reports say our people are riled. I believe that as a sovereign, these concerns should be a priority."

"Do not tell me" —his tenor lowered with each word— "what is a sovereign priority."

"For me, Roman. I can help. I want to help. Your mother..."

"My mother?"

"The queen is growing tired. I could help her, assist her in her work."

"And you believe because the baroness frolics from event to event, that is what you should be doing?"

The small hairs on the back of my neck were standing to attention. "My mother does more than frolic. She raises millions of dollars with her events. That money funds her foundation, which in turn funds—"

"Your father's political agenda."

My eyes opened wide. "Excuse me, sir. My mother's foundation is not a funnel for my father's use."

Roman smirked. "If it were up to me, Edwin would rein in the baroness. She takes far too much of his spotlight."

Through gritted teeth, I maintained my tone. "I'm sure my father would be open to hearing your advice."

"Hearing and heeding are not the same. You hear me, yet you persist with your outlandish ideas."

Outlandish.

Healthcare and essential supplies were far from outlandish. The queen and I had discussed my taking a bigger part, and still, without King Theodore's or Roman's approval, I was not able to assist.

Slowly, Roman turned my direction. "What were you and the princess snickering about?"

Snickering.

I sat tall and spoke slowly. "If you're asking me to recall each conversation I've had throughout the day, I'm unable."

"You are a princess, not a schoolgirl. What you do and say reflects on me."

The moon to his sun.

That wasn't a saying I made up or believed due to Roman's radiating warmth. No, it was told to me by the queen, his mother. My duty was to be a reflection of my husband. The problem was that Roman Godfrey wasn't the sun. He didn't radiate anything worth reflecting.

Another nod and I stared straight ahead, my mind concentrating on maintaining civility, getting back to the plane, debriefing with Lady Buckingham, and readying for bed. Tomorrow we were on to Madrid.

The limousine entered the restricted tarmac where

the royal plane was guarded. Unlike when we arrived, there would not be an audience other than our staff. While those members of our staff and our advisors were blessed with eyes and ears, when it came to our personal lives, they were sworn to keep blind and deaf.

By the time the car came to a stop, there was a line of royal guards on each side of the stairs descending from the plane. Lady Buckingham; Elizabeth Drake, Molave's chief minister; and Lord Avery, Roman's chief assistant, were also present.

Once the door was opened and Roman and I were standing on the tarmac, he leaned down, his liquor-scented breath on my neck. "Advise Lady Buckingham that you will be joining me tonight in my bedchamber."

As our advisors bowed their heads, we ascended the steps.

Once Roman and I were aboard the aircraft, Lord Avery and Mrs. Drake were the next to enter.

"Your Royal Highness," Roman's assistant said, speaking to the prince. "If we may, sir, Mrs. Drake and I request to speak with you before you retire."

My mouth grew dry, wondering if their discussion would include the negative reports I'd only briefly seen. Before agreeing to the discussion, Roman turned my way. "I'll send for you."

Moving one shoe behind the other, I curtsied. "Your Highness."

As the three went one direction, Lady Buckingham appeared at my side. "I'll draw your bath."

No secrets.

No spontaneity.

No choices.

CHAPTER
4

Oliver

My suitcase lay open on my unmade large bed. Slowly it was being filled with clothes, accessories, and toiletries. It wasn't simple to pack for an unknown duration and unforeseen engagements. While walking through my office, I saw the script for the final franchise movie—correction, for *my* final one. Holding it in my grasp, I let it hover over the wastebasket, ready to drop it and listen to the clink as it hit the bottom.

No, the warlord wouldn't do that.

I placed the script on the bookshelf near the others. If all other means of employment failed, I could sell them.

During our call earlier, Ricardo offered to let me crash at his apartment until I made definite plans. I wanted to say I would stay at a hotel in the theater district. That was what the notorious warlord would have done.

Yeah, he was dead.

Despite most of the world and fandom not knowing it, I did.

At some point in thirty-eight years of life, a man comes to expect self-reliance. That meant no crashing on a friend's couch or spare room. I didn't squander all my earnings—I wasn't destitute. And as I was later reminded, I would continue to receive merchandising royalties from my likeness. Andrew called from the airport to remind me of that particular clause in my contract. It meant while the warlord was no more, he could live on in action figures and posters in the bedrooms of fans.

Nevertheless, with my uncertain professional future staring me in the face, I accepted Ricardo's invitation. My airline ticket was purchased. Tomorrow morning, I was flying to New York.

I'd thought of most everything for my time away.

Mrs. Walker, the woman next door, had a key to my place, promising to water my plants—I only had one that was still alive.

A cactus.

It wouldn't dominate her time.

She also promised to collect my mail, which mostly consisted of flyers, and do whatever she could until I returned.

The thing that ate at me was if I wanted to return.

If I find work back on Broadway, do I want to return to the sound stages in Hollywood?

I told myself this wasn't me letting asshole Ronald Estes get to me. If I left California for good, he'd think he'd won. He'd be wrong. If I left the West Coast, it would be for a future somewhere else.

The phone plugged into a charger near my bed began to vibrate. I'd turned off the sound by afternoon. News of my demise was out among my co-stars and the different crews. Everyone was sworn to secrecy, but that didn't stop them from calling and messaging their condolences.

Shit, it was as if the mighty warlord really had died.

Turning the screen upward, I read the name.

Blame it on the coffee with whiskey that morphed into whiskey straight, no chaser, but seeing Rita's name on the screen fueled the gnawing questions I'd fostered since Andrew's visit.

"Hey," I said, by way of answering.

"Oliver, I promise the rumors aren't true."

While it wasn't even five o'clock, my daily nutrients were skewed toward over the limit on alcohol. "I heard they were."

"You think that I'd do that to you, to your career?"

"I didn't say it was you. Is that your conscience talking?"

Her voice grew hushed. "We—you and I—were never exclusive."

"Nope." I supposed the words had never been said. Implied.

Yes, it was implied.

Rita went on, "I was seeing you and Ron at the same time, but I'd never interfere with your livelihood. Tell me that you believe me."

Sitting on the edge of the bed, I held tightly to the phone. "You're a fucking great actor, Rita. I wonder how many times I was the one to witness a performance...a personal performance." Before she could respond, I went on, "Did you ever orgasm? Or was that another role? Fuck, you know if the franchise decides to kill you too, you should try porn."

"Fuck you, Oliver. I called because I care. I didn't give Ron an ultimatum about you. He gave me one about you."

Figures.

"My memory," I said, "is a bit fuzzy, but I'm pretty sure I broke it off with you."

"I know."

"What are you saying? You telling me that Estes gave you an ultimatum and you chose me? It sure as fuck doesn't seem that way."

"I chose you," she said.

My head spun with her declaration.

"Tomorrow," Rita went on, "the cast is getting together at Brett's place in Malibu. Please come."

"I'm headed out of town."

"You can't leave. Come to Brett's and work the room. There's more than one universe out there."

Exhaling, I lay back upon the crumpled sheets and blankets, narrowly missing landing my head in the suitcase. Staring up at the ceiling, I made a decision. I would get on the plane tomorrow and explore what—if anything—there was for me in live performing. Memories returned—the smell of the greasepaint, presence of an audience, and roar of the applause. The energy before the curtain rises. The electricity of having one chance to do the scene right.

I was ready to embrace it.

"Oliver? Are you still there?"

"If you didn't tell Estes it was either you or me, then he made that decision. He chose you, Rita. Live with it. You're involved either way. I already have my ticket for tomorrow. I'll be back for the premiere."

"I hope you find what you're looking for."

"I'm not sure what that is." The whiskey was making me sentimental. "You too. Don't waste your life and talent on a slime like Estes. And for the record, you'd be great at porn."

Rita laughed. "You, too. Stay in touch."

Disconnecting the call, I dropped the phone to the bed and closed my eyes.

When I opened them, the world outside the windows was dark and my empty stomach was growling for real sustenance. Groaning, I blinked my eyes and focused on the half-packed suitcase.

Shit.

Tomorrow, I would be in New York. A thirty-eight-year-old man was about to crash in his friend's apartment in the West Village. Getting up from the bed, I made my way to the kitchen and searched my refrigerator for anything. Somehow eating cereal for dinner reminded me of the old sitcom *Seinfeld.*

Did that show have laugh tracks?

Before I poured the milk, I went back in the bedroom for my phone. Surely, laugh tracks were something I could research. Whoever thought they were a good idea was crazy. It was insulting to the audience and equally as bad as the days when people would lift signs telling the live audience when to applaud. If the script and actors didn't elicit the correct response, the problem wasn't with the audience.

"Shit."

There were multiple missed messages from Andrew, along with a line of text messages from my former castmates. I hit the voicemail symbol.

"Oliver, answer your fucking phone. I don't care when you get this message, call me."

I couldn't recall the destination of my agent's recent trip. Hell, it could be three hours later wherever he was. I was considering waiting until morning to return his call when I saw his latest text message.

"How is your Molavian accent?"

What the hell?

Going back to the kitchen, I returned Andrew's call. As I poured the milk over my dry cereal, the call connected.

"Molave?" I asked, recalling the scene earlier on television.

The sound of people in the background dimmed. "Don't hang up, Oliver. This is a serious offer and she contacted me."

Serious offer.

"That's what you said about the universe."

"Yeah, I'm not saying this is a lifelong gig. I'm saying there is significant earning potential."

"I'd gotten myself psyched up about performing live," I admitted, or maybe I was hoping if I said it, it would be true.

"This is live."

"Who requested me?" I asked before shoving a spoonful of cereal into my mouth.

"Her name is Elizabeth Drake."

"Should I know who she is?"

"From now on, yes," he replied. "Elizabeth Drake is the chief minister to the Godfreys of Molave."

"Your timing is uncanny. I just saw the prince and princess on TV today."

"I'm waiting for my flight back to LAX. Don't leave for New York. I want you to hear the details of this offer from me—in person. And I hope you're dressed. Dustin Hargraves will be to your apartment in a half hour."

I shook my head. "Andrew, what the hell are you talking about?"

"Go to your computer and pull up a photograph of the crown prince of Molave, the Duke of Monovia."

"I saw him today."

"Humor me."

"Shit," I mumbled as I begrudgingly left the remainder of my cereal to get soggy and stepped into my office. It took me two tries to spell Molave, but finally I got it. "Okay, I'm looking at him."

"And what do you see?"

"Fuck, a miserable, entitled lunatic who according to this article is not enhancing Molave's foreign relations." I clicked the arrow bringing up a picture of the prince with his wife, Princess Lucille. "Damn, she's something else. I'd say the prince outplayed his coverage."

"Back to the prince. Don't you see it?"

"What do you want me to see?"

"He looks like you. You look like him," Andrew said.

My eyes narrowed as I studied the prince's face. "I mean, I guess. He's five years older than I am, and there's gray in his hair." Not a lot, but some. I looked at the photo of him in a uniform. "I'd say he also weighs more than me."

"Fine, you're not twins separated at birth, but the resemblance is enough that the royal family wants to hire you to take on some of the prince's obligations. I'll tell you more when I get to your place."

"I have a ticket for New York. I've spoken with Ricardo."

"Oliver," Andrew said. "Listen to me. This is an opportunity of a lifetime. The Firm is offering to pay double what you made for the last movie."

"Double?" I sighed, leaning back in the chair. "For how long?"

"Cancel your ticket to New York."

I thought about the suitcase. "I'm mostly packed."

"Good, because you'll be heading to Molave."

"I haven't said yes."

"You will. And one more thing."

"What?"

"Don't tell a soul. This must stay confidential. You don't want to cross the royal family."

CHAPTER
5

Lucille

"I am the princess," I proclaimed with as much authority as I could muster. "I summoned you here to tell me why I haven't been in contact with the prince. I also want to know more about the reported food shortages in various regions of Molave."

"Not all reports are accurate."

"Mrs. Drake, I'm reporting that I've barely spoken to my husband in weeks. That is accurate. As for the reports of food shortages, I took a tour of the western province yesterday. The grocer's shelves were nearly empty."

Stone-faced with resolve, Molave's chief minister, Mrs. Drake, stood before me. The only comment that caused a micro-expression was news of my tour. In the hierarchy that existed, I was above her. The unspoken reality was quite different. Mrs. Drake had access that I did not. She held closed-door meetings with King Theodore and Prince Roman.

"That isn't your concern," she replied. "It would be

better if you didn't voice those thoughts publicly or in private with the queen or king."

Yesterday, when I sent an email to Mrs. Drake, I also sent one to the queen. The one sent to the queen hadn't been returned, and as for the chief minister, she was now here, in the province of Monovia at Annabella Castle.

Perhaps her presence was the answer from both correspondents. Mrs. Drake worked closely with the advisors to the royal family, affectionately referred to by many as 'the Firm.'

I'd first heard the term during my pre-marriage exercises. It wasn't my husband-to-be who mentioned it. The nickname came from Roman's sister, Princess Isabella. While we didn't exactly become quick friends, over the last few years, Isabella and I had established a rapport of sorts. Perhaps it was more of an understanding; nevertheless, it existed.

Molave had yet to follow other monarchies around the world in recognizing females as equal to males in their birthright. It wouldn't matter if Molave did. Isabella was five years younger than Roman. Which meant she was five years older than I.

Currently, thirty-eight years of age, Isabella had been married to the Duke of Wilmington since weeks before Roman's and my first anniversary. I later learned the princess had been forbidden to marry prior to her older brother.

If everything went as planned, one day I would be queen. The only way Isabella could ascend to that title would be in the case of Roman's passing and that of our children—the ones we don't yet have—and even then, it would require her husband, the duke, to renounce his duchy of Wilmington, a region outside the Molave state.

Due to conflicts of interests between the two countries, there had been discussion of renouncing the duke's title prior to their marriage. I wasn't privy to how the dilemma was settled, only that the two married, somehow keeping Francis's title intact.

While regent titles may never be bestowed upon Isabella and Francis, in the heir department, the Duke and Duchess of Wilmington wasted no time in producing their heir and a spare.

Turning away from Mrs. Drake, I peered out the library's large windows. The castle grounds beyond the panes were brightening with autumn colors. The summer heat was gone. Our Eurasia tour was over a month past, and from what I was able to glean, it had been a humanitarian and public relations success.

Foreign relations were given a less favorable rating.

Roman's ideals were not in alignment with his father's. The people of Molave as well as neighboring royalty didn't always approve of my husband's outspoken ways.

Once we returned to Monovia, Roman was summoned to the palace in Molave City. That was nearly a fortnight ago. I had only spoken to him a few times on the phone since then. The walls of Annabella Castle, where we called home, were beginning to close in around me, much like the choker I'd worn in London.

"Your Highness."

I nodded toward the seat opposite me in my formal library.

Mrs. Drake curtsied before taking the chair. "The Duke of Monovia is resting."

"Resting? Why isn't he resting here in our home?"

"The royal family is making every effort to keep up appearances." She leaned closer, lowering her volume. "The Duke's success is essential for Molave's future. Especially with the king's age, the duke has been under a tremendous pressure. That pressure has at times been reported as disagreement within the family. As you know, that isn't the case."

Sitting properly with my ankles crossed and my hands daintily in my lap, I made the same plea to Mrs. Drake that had fallen on deaf ears with Roman. "I want to help, ma'am."

"Your Highness?"

Exhaling, I lowered my chin and steadied my expression. "I read many of the news breaks regarding our tour."

"You really shouldn't believe—"

"While I was relegated to photo opportunities," I said, interrupting, "those endeavors were met with praise. If I could speak to King Theodore, I would implore him that allowing his daughter-in-law, the country's princess, to be an ambassador for Molave in a more substantial role than that of subservient wife would send a strong signal to the world."

A few of the news sources had been downright cruel regarding projections of Roman's wellness—physical and mental. Despite my personal feelings concerning my husband, I had once cared for him. I had made an obligation to be his wife. The way he grew rigid in public, was obviously distracted, and quick to disagree also had me worried. It was what I wanted to ask him about after our dinner at Buckingham Palace.

Roman despised weakness.

I knew that.

And while he wouldn't admit there was anything going on with him, it was visible to more than just me.

That perception of infirmity was why no matter what occurred behind closed doors, I maintained my strength in and out of his presence. Truly, I disliked the man I married, but I would take my vows to my grave and support him, the family, and the country.

Mrs. Drake sat unyielding, her neck rigidly straight and her lips pressed into a straight line. Her short hair contained a peppering of gray that on a man would be considered distinguished. The purple pantsuit she wore contrasted nicely with her black blouse and string of ivory pearls. Despite her position in the royal firm, the chief minister wore the customary heeled shoes and carried a small clutch that all females had.

It could go without mentioning that Elizabeth Drake had worked diligently to get to her position. Molave was not a shining beacon in the world of gender equality.

"Your Highness," she said placatingly, "if you were to step in and do the prince's duties, it would appear as if he were incapable."

Is he?

I didn't ask that.

"Or, ma'am," I countered, "perhaps it would demonstrate that the king sees both of us as capable."

"The family has taken steps to reduce the prince's stressors."

Taking a breath, I stood, paced near the windows, and turned. "Mrs. Drake, I will be frank. Roman is my husband and my place is as his helper. Stuck in this castle by myself is not a way for me to fulfill my role or my duties as his wife or this country's princess." I lifted my chin. "If you're unable to help me reach Roman or King Theodore, I will have no other choice than to reach out myself."

"You're not alone."

"No. You're right. I'm well taken care of. I asked for your audience to emphasize to you, woman to woman, that I am available to do whatever I am asked— and even what is not asked."

Mrs. Drake nodded. "I will take your pleas back to the king."

Walking toward my desk, I picked up my schedule for the day and then shuffled to one for the week. I lifted my chin, meeting Mrs. Drake's gaze. "Friday, Duchess Isabella is celebrating Rothy's second birthday at the palace in Molave City. I will be there."

"Yes, well, that was one of the items I came to Annabella Castle to discuss with you face-to-face. Your presence won't be required."

"Required?" My volume rose. "It is a birthday party for a two-year-old boy. Attendance is not required, it is requested, and I have accepted."

"Your acceptance has been overruled." Mrs. Drake inhaled and stood with a curtsy. "Princess Lucille, when you agreed to marry the crown prince, you did so with the understanding that you were subject to the royal family. At this juncture, the royal family is asking for your patience."

My patience had expired long before the disastrous Eurasia tour, long before my husband's struggle for power found one outlet—me. That particular component of our marriage was the one reason why up until yesterday seeing the food shortages, I hadn't pushed to reunite with Prince Roman.

"What is being done about the food shortages?" I asked.

"Perceived, Your Highness. It's simply a matter of distribution."

In a country the size of Molave, the majority of commerce was imported. Our country's energy went to refining the natural resources for export. The exports created wealth that didn't coincide with hunger.

"Yesterday, in the western province, I entered a grocer's," I said. "Empty shelves were visible not perceived."

"Are you without any of your amenities, Your Highness? Do you lack food," —she looked around the palatial library— "shelter, medical attention?"

"I do not. Neither should the citizens of Molave."

"There have been some tensions in mining. It's a wrinkle. Another stress on the prince."

Mining.

"If I may," Mrs. Drake said, "I am needed back in the capital. I will take your concerns to the royal family. I would urge you not to leave the castle grounds as you did yesterday. There has been a bit of an upheaval, and your safety is paramount. Another reason why traveling to a child's birthday celebration is ill-advised."

I pressed the button on the table near my chair. "Mrs. Drake," I said through clenched teeth, with a nod of my head.

The door to the library opened as Geoffrey, one of the castle butlers, entered.

"Your Highness." A nod and a curtsy, and Mrs. Drake was gone.

"Tell Lady Buckingham," I spoke to Geoffrey, "I wish for her audience."

"Yes, Your Highness," he said with a bow.

As he stepped away, I hurried to my laptop and began to type.

First, I tried *Unrest in Molave.*

The circle spun and spun, but nothing materialized.

Second, *Food shortages.*

Multiple articles appeared with news from around the globe, but nothing in Molave.

I was typing in: *Mining tensions Molave* as there was a knock and Lady Buckingham entered.

My gaze met hers. "Is access by my computers restricted?"

She curtsied and came closer. "Your Highness?"

"I can't read any of the news about Molave."

"What news?"

"Anything. I can access North America, the United States. I even see an article about King Felipe VI in Spain." My pulse began to race with each spin of the circle on my screen. "Here is something about a coup in Istanbul and an article about Borinkia." My gaze met hers. "How long has this been happening?"

Lady Buckingham's expression sobered. "The information available to you has always been vetted."

"What?"

"Only since the recent tour has it become more restricted."

I slapped the top of the table. "I read about the reactions to the prince."

She nodded. "While we were out of the country, yes. The vetting is more difficult outside the grounds of Annabella Castle. Since our return, you have been shielded."

Shielded.

"This is bullshit."

"Your Highness," she said with a hint of admonishment.

"Lady Buckingham, have my things packed.

Tomorrow, I'm headed to the palace in Molave City to see my husband and attend Prince Rothy's birthday gathering."

"I was instructed—"

"I am going," I said with every ounce of determination. "And we will not announce my travel until it is underway. Is that clear?"

Lady Buckingham acquiesced with a bow of her head and a mention of my name.

Turning back to the windows, I stared out at the colorful leaves as my thoughts spun with questions, wondering what I'd missed while locked away.

CHAPTER
6

Lucille

Billowing clouds filled the early autumn skies as pouring rain created streams flowing through the castle lawns. Staring out the window of my private suite, I held tight to the warm cup of tea and watched the scene with morbid fascination. Despite the latitudinal position of Molave, the influence of the North Atlantic Ocean made the southern region of our country much warmer than the latitudinal position would indicate. The most noticeable change as winter approached was the lack of daylight. In the summer months, there were few hours of darkness. Soon, it will be the opposite.

I spun toward the door at the sound of Lady Buckingham's knock.

A curtsy and a bow of her head, and she came closer, shutting the door behind her. "Your Highness, the palace guards have been made aware that there is a restriction on your travel."

My things were packed and all that separated me

from the palace in Molave City was a two-hour drive through the mountains to the coast.

"By?"

"Senior guards in Molave City."

"Nonsense," I said, shaking my head and setting the teacup back upon the saucer. "Only the monarchs have the authority to overrule me." After five years, I'd learned a thing or two. "Unless the decision is directly from the prince, queen, or king, I am traveling."

"Mrs. Drake—"

"Does not have the authority."

"No, Your Highness. The chief minister warned of danger. It would be best not to travel alone—in one car," she clarified.

Bending rules wasn't the same as breaking them.

"Instead of the royal fleet," I proposed, "we will travel in a few separate automobiles unmarked with the royal standard. No one will know it is us."

"You will have to be announced in order to receive admission to the palace grounds."

"And at that time," I said, "I will already be there. Surely, you don't believe the guards would turn me away—with safety concerns."

"If I could reach out to the queen's mistress?"

I shook my head.

As last night progressed, I became more and more upset with Mrs. Drake's visit. Damn the consequences,

I wanted to know what was happening. Staying safe behind walls and gates wouldn't allow me to learn what was underway.

"Inform me when the automobiles are ready."

Lady Buckingham bowed before going to the tray that had been brought to me for breakfast. As she was about to lift the silver dome, I went toward her and laid my hand on top.

"Lucille?"

"I'm not hungry, and I don't plan to waste time talking about what I have or haven't consumed. Once we're to Molave City, I will eat."

Lady Buckingham's lips pressed together. Her gray eyes told me she didn't approve, yet her words stayed silent.

As she carried the tray toward the door, I said, "You will ride with me."

With an upturn of her lips, she nodded. "Of course, ma'am."

Despite the hushed whispers as Lady Buckingham and I entered the first car, my plan was in full motion. The earlier rain was now a drizzle as we were driven through the first castle gate. The long brick lane that led away from the castle was covered by a canopy of tree limbs. Leaves from above fell, floating to the ground and covering the lane in a slippery mixture.

As the final gate opened, the car didn't move

forward. With a quick look ahead, I saw the reason. A small crowd of people stood, chanting and blocking our way.

My pulse increased as Lady Buckingham reached for my hand.

"What is happening?" I asked. "It wasn't like this two days ago."

"Your Highness," our driver said, "I should take you back to Annabella Castle."

"No," I replied, listening to the words from beyond the windows.

In the royal fleet, the doors were thicker, the windows also. I'd requested normal cars. That was what I had.

"Princess, help us."

They were calling to me.

My forehead furrowed as I turned to Lady Buckingham. "I should speak."

"No, Your Highness, you should not." She held tighter to my hand. "It isn't safe."

"Put the car in park," I demanded.

As the driver complied, the people moved closer, entering the castle grounds. Our driver radioed to the guards in the cars following behind. I waited until the guards secured a space beyond my door. "Tell him to open it," I said.

My driver sent the message.

I wasn't dressed for a photo op. On the contrary, I was wearing traveling clothes: slacks, boots, and a jumper covered by a long mackintosh. Summoning my determination, I took a deep breath as the door opened.

The light drizzle fell to my hair as I stepped out. The loud chants quieted as people bowed and curtsied and murmurs of my name filled my ears.

Taking a step beyond my guard, I approached a woman. Wearing a dark mac and a plastic bonnet covering her white hair, she was soaked to the skin. I reached for her, and her chilled hands trembled in my grasp.

"Hello."

The older woman managed a curtsy before grasping my hand. "Princess Lucille."

Nodding, I looked at her and around at the others. The entire crowd was watching the two of us. "You will catch your death out here in this weather."

"The young prince's birthday, Your Highness. We've been here since yesterday morning, hoping to see you before you went to the palace."

"I'm here. What do you want of me?"

Her eyes opened wide as the crowd took a collective breath.

"I want to know why you're waiting," I said with a sad smile. "How may I help?"

"We" —she looked around to the others— "come to

you, humbly asking that you will please speak to King Theodore."

"I shall, I'm certain."

"The prince's tariffs."

"His tariffs?" I didn't mean for it to sound like a question.

"Do you not know?" a man close by asked rather loudly.

"I'm sorry, no."

The crowd grew louder.

Letting go of the woman's hand, I lifted mine. "Please. I don't know about the tariffs, but not because I don't want to. I do. I'm headed to the palace in Molave City to take my place and represent each of you."

"King Theodore has approved this?" the man from a moment ago asked.

"You have my word I'll speak to the king."

"Word is," the older woman said, "the king is ill. He must know what the crown prince has done."

"I will do all I can," I said.

The discontentment eased as the crowd bowed their heads and offered words of appreciation.

"If you'll allow us to pass," I said. The air filled with chants of Princess Lucille.

Once I was back inside the car, I turned to Lady

Buckingham. "I think our plan of arriving unannounced was for naught."

"Perhaps you should place a call..."

My empty stomach twisted with dread for my first conversation with my husband. If he knew what had just occurred, he wouldn't take my call. If he didn't know, it was better to not rush his anger.

"To the palace," I said. "I will speak with the prince in person." I turned to my mistress and lowered my voice. "What do you know of the king's health?"

She shook her head. "Only rumors."

My chest twisted.

King Theodore was respected by the people of Molave, by those beyond the borders as well. Despite his title and power, he'd always been kind to me, even jovial. Yes, I'd speak to my husband, and also to the king.

CHAPTER 7

Oliver

The apartment within a long wing of the third floor of the Molave palace made my condo in Hollywood look like a tenement house. For the last three weeks-plus, I had been living the life of a crown prince. There was a small entourage who were aware of my presence. Those people bowed and curtsied. They addressed me by titles such as your highness, duke, or prince. They were omnipresent in my preparation by immersion.

Within the palace, I was hidden and treated like a king, or a king to be.

My assistants and servants taught me how to stand, what to say, and how to respond.

In the last three and a half weeks, I'd read volumes on the Duke of Monovia. I'd already had one outing where I didn't speak but was driven to a location where I waved to the crowd as I entered the building. An hour later, I repeated the performance as I exited.

There was no inkling that I was an impostor.

Gone were my blue jeans and canvas loafers.

Now I wore suits with a padded shirt beneath, giving me a similar shape to the man I was paid to impersonate.

Without a doubt, this was the craziest assignment I'd ever taken.

"Your Highness," Lord Martin, my chief assistant, said with a bow of his head as he entered my apartment.

Lord Martin didn't know my birth name, but he knew I wasn't the crown prince of Monovia. From what I'd been able to learn, he and the others assigned to me were sworn to secrecy and well compensated.

"Yes?"

He tilted his head. "Not a question, sir."

"Yes."

He nodded. "Tomorrow is the birthday of Rothy, the son of the Duke and Duchess of Wilmington."

"My sister, Princess Isabella, and her husband, Francis."

"Very good, sir. I have been informed that Prince Roman is unable to attend."

My breath caught as I felt the blood drain from my face. "They want me to attend a child's birthday party with close family? Surely, in the presence of family, I will be discovered." And then what...death?

I'd been assured that wouldn't be the case; nevertheless, the more I learned the rules and customs of this sovereign country, the less secure I felt.

"If I may."

That phrase was what Lord Martin and Lady Caroline said as a prelude to any tidbits of knowledge I would need.

"Go on." Truly my accent was improving. At first, I sounded as if I were a Norwegian caught in Wales with a Scottish ancestor. In other words, it was bad. However, I'd spent hours each day working virtually with Andrew's voice coach, Dustin Hargraves. Between those lessons, the conversations with Lord Martin and Lady Caroline, and speaking fluent Norwegian, I was improving.

"You, sir, are not close to your sister or your brother-in-law. You have only met your nephew on two occasions. The child will not realize you are different. As for your sister and brother-in-law, remain aloof. After an appearance for the palace photographers, you will be summoned and leave."

"What about King Theodore or Queen Anne?"

"Your father, the king, is not feeling well. He will not be in attendance. The queen will be present. Carry on with small talk and if this goes well, the chief minister believes you will be ready to take a stronger role."

"And if it doesn't?"

Lord Martin bowed his head. When he looked up, there was an unusual smile on his lips. "Not a question, sir."

Taking a deep breath, I let my chest expand. I'd spent hours watching palace videos and news clips. Mimicking the prince's movements and common gestures was much easier than making small talk with his mother.

"What of Princess Lucille?"

"She will not be in attendance."

While that news made me more confident in my success, I found I was also disappointed. In the videos I'd viewed, I found myself watching her more than Roman. There was something I couldn't put my finger on about their interaction. At times, I wanted to reach through the screen and grab Roman by the neck of his shirt and tell him to look at her, to see her and acknowledge her.

It was as if being acknowledged was all the princess wanted. In the many hours of tapes I'd watched, I rarely—if ever—saw that need met.

"Your Highness," Lord Martin said, "I will return with recent happenings for your small talk and information about your sister's family."

"You're dismissed."

Lord Martin bowed his head and turned toward the door. Before he reached for the handle, he turned back with a grin. "Well done, sir. Your tone is sounding more impatient."

"May I confess I'm not a fan of the impatient, entitled attitude?"

"No, Your Highness, you may not. It is who you are when you are he."

I waved my hand. "Be gone."

"Yes, sir."

* * *

"If the queen mentions the reported food shortages, assure her emphatically and impatiently that the rumors are poppycock," Lord Martin said as he dressed me for the birthday celebration.

"I address the Queen as Mum."

Lord Martin nodded.

My thoughts went to the food shortage topic. "I've seen the empty shelves on the television."

"Telly, sir."

"Quite right," I said, "on the telly."

"Reassure her majesty that those reports are fabrications, exaggerations by the anti-royal media. You have the situation covered."

Lord Martin took a step back and smiled. "Yes, Your Royal Highness, you look like him."

Turning, I took in my reflection in the full-length

mirror. My hair had grown out since I arrived and now had the addition of a sprinkling of gray. The padded shirt gave me the appearance of an extra twenty-five pounds. Holding my shoulders back and my chin up, I could almost believe the man in the mirror was the crown prince of Molave.

"Splendid, sir," Lord Martin said.

My gaze met his. "Do I?"

"Resemble the prince? Yes."

"No, do I have the food shortages covered?"

"Matters of state, Your Highness."

I recalled the report I'd watched this morning on the telly. There was an amateur video of Princess Lucille talking to people outside Annabella Castle. Not only did the report not make it sound as if the situation was handled, but there were also prognosticators who believed it would get worse. Something about retaliatory tariffs in response to a mining strike.

"Are you ready, Your Highness?"

This moment was the exhilaration of the curtain raising, with the added stress of a private audience. "I am." And then I slipped into character. "Let's get this over with. I have better ways to spend my time."

Lord Martin nodded with a grin.

As we navigated the hallways, walking where I had never been, Lord Martin refreshed my memory on etiquette. I bowed only to the king and queen.

Everyone else was in a state of subjugation to me, even my wife.

My steps stopped. "You said the princess wouldn't be in attendance."

"There has been a change of plans."

"Certainly, you don't believe I can fool his wife."

"Aloof, sir, and *your* wife. The two of you have had words. There's no need for more."

Something within my chest twisted. "Words? Are you saying Roman wouldn't speak to his wife?"

In lieu of answering, Lord Martin whispered as he opened a tall door, "The celebration is beyond this dining room."

We both stopped in our tracks as the most stunning blue eyes opened wide at our presence before being veiled with long lashes and looking down. The princess dipped in an exaggerated curtsy. The sight of her in person took my breath away, making my heart beat in triple time.

"Your Highness," Princess Lucille said before our gazes met.

"Lucille." It was unscripted. Up until moments ago, I never dreamt we'd be face-to-face. Now that we were, I witnessed the same expression I'd seen in the films.

Her voice was a melody. "I will go back to Monovia following the celebration as I promised."

Leave?

Why did they want her gone?

Was it because of me?

"Your Highness," Lord Martin said, speaking to me.

Inflating my chest as I'd been instructed to do, I spoke, "Lord Martin, leave us."

"Sir, we should—"

I waved my hand. As Lord Martin stepped away through the door to the celebration, I turned my attention to Princess Lucille.

"Your Highness," she said, the pink drained from her cheeks. "I am sorry about the news reports. I realize how riled you rightfully are. It won't happen again. As I said yesterday, it is my duty to be here, for you and for Isabella."

Our relationship, or that of her and her husband, had not been explained to me. We weren't supposed to meet.

Her words faded as I watched her lips, luscious and pink.

There was an attraction or pull that I couldn't explain as I moved toward her step by step. The long-sleeved yellow dress she wore covered her flesh, but her curves were on full display. However, my concentration was on her beautiful face. The deep blue of her eyes, the sculpture of her cheekbones, and the pertness of her nose led me back to her kissable lips.

As her melody of a voice continued to explain and apologize, I sensed a strong, formidable woman lurking beneath the surface. I couldn't stop myself as I gently reached for her cheek and brushed her lips with mine.

Sweet as honey, our kiss began tentatively. Much like a simmering pot of water, as our kiss lingered and the heat grew, the rolling boil came to life. Lucille's breathing hitched as the rigidity of her posture melted, pressing her softness against my chest. Even through the padded shirt, I sensed her warmth, her passion, and her desire. Soft mews filled my ears as I wrapped my arm around her waist, tugging her closer.

I was completely lost in this stunning woman until my mind overruled the attraction.

This was another man's wife.

Releasing her, I took a step back.

As if embarrassed or ashamed, Lucille looked up at me with her widened eyes. Her cheeks were pink and her lips swollen.

I'd been discovered.

Before the celebration even began, I'd been discovered for the impostor I was.

I had to do something.

Straightening my stance, I lowered my tenor. "You're my wife. No further explanation is necessary."

Nodding, Lucille quickly curtsied.

Offering her my arm, despite the thumping of my pulse, I forced my smile to dim. "Shall we?"

"Your Highness?"

"I will escort my" —I wanted to say wife, but she wasn't mine— "princess."

Lucille laid her petite hand upon my arm and looked up at me. "I feel as if I don't know you anymore."

CHAPTER
8

Lucille

Yesterday upon my arrival, Roman was riled, even ruthless in his admonishment of my behavior. I'd disobeyed the family's order to stay in Monovia. I'd pointed out that the chief minister was not the family. If Roman wanted me to stay at Annabella Castle, then he could have called me. I knew I was playing with fire. It seemed the more I was left to my own devices, the more I pushed.

I wanted a reaction.

Even fire was preferable to drought.

The reaction I received was not unexpected, yet it was a response.

Our encounter stayed verbal until Lord Avery showed Roman a video shot outside Annabella Castle of me speaking to the crowd. It was then the prince ordered Lord Avery to leave us. As red seeped upward from his thick neck, I awaited what was to come next.

As if Roman Godfrey had taken on a Jekyll-and-Hyde persona, the man who rebuked me yesterday was the Hyde to this Jekyll, the man whose lips and touch were awakening a part of me I'd thought dead.

In my husband's embrace, my forgotten desires made themselves known. The tightening of my nipples, twisting of my core, and dampness of my bloomers weren't foreign, and yet it had been too long since I'd had this reaction.

The complete one-hundred-and-eighty-degree turn of my emotions had my mind and body in an unexpected battle. My mind cautioned me to be wary and to question what was real. My body had other ideas.

This unexpected sensation began the moment my gaze met Roman's. It seemed as if he were looking at me anew. I almost questioned that it was the man I married or if I was conjuring up a substitute in my mind.

I wondered if I could have imagined the change in my reaction into being, as if wishing would make it real. My mind told me not to hope. It only brought disappointment. And then Roman cupped my cheek, stilling my long-winded apology.

My apprehension melted as Roman wrapped his arm around me. His lips took mine, his kiss strong, even possessive, yet it wasn't forced or rough. In the seconds we connected, all my reservations about this man faded away. The dining room where soon the staff would present the birthday meal was forgotten. The celebration itself was gone from my thoughts as I molded against the man I remembered.

It was as Roman abruptly stopped our kiss that I realized whatever had just occurred was not his intention. Gone were his smile and the glint in his brown eyes. Back were his rigid posture and staunch expression.

It was his words that continued the shock waves that began with his earthquaking kiss.

"You're my wife. No further explanation is necessary."

My eyes opened wider as I fought to understand his meaning. Questions spiraled in my mind as I nodded and curtsied.

Was the subject of my disobedience truly closed?

Did he not expect me to further subjugate myself?

When I looked up, Roman was offering me his arm. "Shall we?"

"Your Highness?" I questioned, unaccustomed to any form of physical contact while in the presence of others, especially the queen.

His voice was deeper than usual, his words more enunciated. "I will escort my" —he paused— "princess."

His princess.

That shouldn't make me swoon, yet it did.

Laying my hand upon the prince's arm, I looked up

at his stare and spoke more freely than I normally would. "I feel as if I don't know you anymore."

His firm lips came together as if there was more he wanted to say.

If I had the power, I would have directed us away from the celebration to the gardens or even upstairs to our apartments. I couldn't pinpoint the change in the man at my side, but for a few minutes, I basked in my husband's adoration as if it were the first rays of sunshine after years of flooding rain.

I wanted more.

Alas, Roman pushed the swinging door, and all eyes turned our direction, including those of the queen.

"Roman," she called, lifting her hand.

Removing my hand, I curtsied. To my astonishment, Roman stayed at my side, his bow at the waist exaggerated before placing his hand in the small of my back and leading me to the queen.

"Mum," he said before kissing her cheek.

"Lucille," she said with a smile. "I'd like a minute with my son."

"Yes, Your Majesty," I dutifully replied with a bow of my head. As I took a step back, Roman's gaze met mine, only for a second before turning back to his mother. It was a connection, one I'd longed for, one I again questioned its reality.

Was I truly so unhappy that I could be creating fiction in my mind?

Blinking, I looked around the large room, finding my bearings. No one else was staring at Roman.

Did anyone else sense a difference?

The answer appeared to be no.

In a confused daze, I made my way across the large parlor to Princess Isabella and the birthday boy, Prince Rothy.

"Thank you for coming," Isabella whispered with a squeeze of my hand. "I know Roman can be overbearing."

I looked across the large room, seeing the back of my husband's head and his shoulders. My vision continued lower until reaching his shoes. I'd smelled the aroma of his cologne, looked into his dark eyes, and still my mind was reeling. I turned back to Isabella and kept my volume low. "Does he seem different?"

"Who?"

"Roman," I responded.

Isabella looked toward Roman, still conversing with the queen. She scoffed. "No, same pompous ass." Her smile returned. "I am glad you're here."

"I wanted to be here for Rothy." I turned to the dark-haired boy on the floor with Duke Francis and back with a grin. "This is his only second birthday."

"I was told you wouldn't be able to travel due to the unrest."

I lowered my volume even more. "I've been sheltered. Would you tell me more about what's happening?"

"You don't know?"

I shook my head in a wordless reply.

Isabella's dark brown eyes opened wider as she too scanned the room. "Not now, but yes, I'll tell you what I know." She leaned closer. "You're unaware and yet you spoke to the crowd outside the castle?"

Nodding, I recalled Roman's displeasure regarding that subject. "Lady Buckingham was right; I shouldn't have spoken. It was impulsive." I shrugged. "I want to help."

"Let me guess, my brother doesn't approve."

I shook my head.

Isabella reached again for my hand. "You're admired by the people." She tilted her chin toward Roman. "He's jealous."

Tears prickled the back of my eyes. "I don't know what to do."

"Don't give up and stay strong."

That was the end of Isabella's sisterly advice as the nanny appeared with Princess Alice. The toddler had turned one year old during the summer. Unlike her brother, Alice's hair was fair, much like her father's, and hanging in soft ringlets.

Soon, the queen and Roman joined us as Rothy unwrapped his gifts, and the royal photographer snapped photos of the monumental event.

While Queen Anne sat on the velvet sofa facing Isabella and me, Roman remained standing off to the side, his arms crossed over his chest. The expression of disinterest was the husband I knew. The way he continually and impatiently checked his watch and let out long sighs were all too familiar.

And then every now and again, I thought I'd caught him looking at me. When I did, instead of getting the feeling that I was in someway not representing him or failing to be the moon to his sun, I felt a rare sense of warmth as if the sun was actually within him.

My mind was playing tricks.

It was as Queen Anne's mistress, Lady Kornhall, announced dinner was to be served that Lord Martin entered and spoke to Roman, too softly to be over-heard. Roman's eyes met mine before he announced his departure to the rest of the room.

Everything within me wanted him to request my presence.

Realizing that I was hoping for something I usually loathed, my chin dropped with the overwhelming disappointment that he didn't. Roman didn't even speak directly to me before turning and leading Lord Martin from the room and away from the dining hall.

My stomach was in knots as the battle raged within me.

It was as if for a moment, I'd stepped through the looking glass to a world where I meant something to the man I vowed to love. His cold departure sent me spiraling back to reality. As I stood to make my way to the dining room, Isabella reached for my arm and whispered, "It's happening again. He's troubled," she clarified. "Don't let him get to you."

Raising my chin, I inhaled. "I'm sorry, Princess, for being transparent. I know it is frowned—"

"Lucille" —her tone was emphatic— "you are a godsend to Roman, to this family. I only ask that you savor the good while tolerating the bad. From what I've been told, Roman's social anxiety is getting worse. He almost didn't make it to the party. I'd been warned he'd leave early."

Social anxiety.

I was aware of his phobia, but in the five years we'd been wed, it seemed to be under control. I knew without a doubt that it was not a subject that he'd discuss. My gaze met my sister-in-law's. "Is that why he hates me? Is it because I am comfortable..." I didn't finish the sentence.

"He doesn't hate you. You're his wife."

That was what he usually told me. A smile threatened to curl my lips at the memory of him saying I was *his* princess. Simple, lovely...and his.

"Your Highnesses, dinner is waiting," Lady Kornhall said with an admonishing tone.

"I'm getting us in trouble," I whispered after a nod to the queen's mistress.

"She's an old fuddy-duddy," Isabella replied with a grin.

Our steps stuttered as we entered the dining room and found King Theodore seated at the head of the table. The royal portraits of Theodore and Anne at the time of their marriage showed the king to be an exceptionally handsome man. Roman took after him in that way. The contrast was starker in their personalities. While today the king's complexion was paler than normal, his smile was still present.

"Your Grace," Isabella and I said in unison with a curtsy.

"Papa," Isabella added after the formal greeting. Hugging his neck, she beamed. "I thought you weren't feeling well."

"And miss the prince's birthday," he replied in his booming tone. "Never."

"Theo," Queen Anne said, "remember what the physician said."

As he waved the queen's reminder off with a hearty laugh, the entire room fell under his spell. I'd heard stories that when in dealings of state, King Theodore was a master and always in control. My experience was on a more personal level—in a word, he was charming.

"Lucille," he said, lifting his hand.

Going to him, I took his hand with a slight curtsy.

"Where is my son?"

"He was here." I looked around to see all eyes on me. "I don't believe he knew you were to attend. I'm sure if he had, he wouldn't have left when he was called away."

Small lines formed near the corners of his brown eyes as he grinned. "Tell him I miss him."

"I shall."

As I made my way to my seat, I wondered if I'd just been given a reason to approach my husband before my departure. After all, it was a mandate from the king himself.

CHAPTER
9

Oliver

Lord Martin and I remained tight-lipped as he led me through the maze back to my apartment. With each step echoing through the empty hallways, the temperature within me rose. It was the combination of the anxiety associated with opening *NYC Broadway Show Reviews* and reading the critic's evaluation of your performance mixed with the reality that I was impersonating a royal in the presence of royals.

Although I was confident in my interaction with the queen, it was Princess Lucille who had me troubled in more ways than my continued employment.

My inner furnace was ablaze by the time we reached the apartment. In the presence of Lord Martin and Lady Caroline, I stripped off my suitcoat, tugged at my tie, and struggled with the buttons on my shirt.

"Your Highness?" Lord Martin questioned with wide eyes.

Undressing me was his duty.

I couldn't wait.

If I didn't get out of these clothes, I would suffocate.

Throwing the suitcoat and tie to the floor, I gave up on the buttons, pulling the front of the shirt apart as small buttons littered the carpeting. I wasn't done. Lifting the padded shirt over my head, I let out a roar as I threw it to the floor.

"Fuck."

The chill of the apartment air contrasted the heat within me that had my undershirt drenched with sweat. Ignoring the two sets of eyes upon me, I stalked to the highboy and poured a glass of still water. It wasn't until I had downed the second glass that I turned to my assistants, ready for their rebuke.

To my surprise, they were both smiling. It wasn't that they were ever animated, but in this case, they both appeared pleased.

"Which one of you is going to say it?"

"Say what, Your Highness?" Lord Martin asked.

"I fucked up."

Lady Caroline walked from one article of clothing to the next, tidying up what I'd left in my wake as Lord Martin clasped his hands behind his back and sighed.

"You didn't" —he paused— "fuck up."

The way he pronounced the common obscenity made me grin.

Lady Caroline stood with an armful of my clothing and a handful of buttons. "If I may?"

"Yes," I replied impatiently, "you always may. Just say it."

"I wasn't present at the celebration. Word is that no one, including the queen, was the wiser." She looked down at the clothes and back to me. "This behavior you just displayed was classic crown prince, sir." She bowed her eyes, veiling her smile. "Minus the extra padding."

"Classic?" I looked from one to the other. "It was childish and uncalled for."

Lord Martin nodded. "You're learning."

"Ridiculous," I muttered. Wearing my trousers and a perspiration-soaked plain white t-shirt, I went to one of the plush chairs and sat. "What about Princess Lucille?"

Lord Martin came closer. "I wasn't in the room. What do you think?"

What do I think?

That was a broad question. In an encounter that lasted no more than a few minutes, I thought Princess Lucille was one of the most beautiful women I'd ever laid eyes on. I felt a yearning emitting from her like sirens through the fog of royal protocol. I'd reacted instinctively instead of as the crown prince.

"I wasn't prepared," I admitted. "We haven't discussed the prince's relationship with his wife."

"Strained, Your Highness," Lady Caroline volunteered.

Strained.

I nodded. "I felt" —I looked up, meeting Lady Caroline's gaze— "a pull. She is..." I searched for the right words. "I've seen her expressions in the hours of videos I've watched. She wants Roman to look at her, to really look at her. In that moment, I wanted to give that to her."

Lady Caroline inhaled and looked to Lord Martin before back to me. "You cannot."

She was correct. I should not. It wasn't my place to give Lucille what Roman should; however, being correct somehow felt wrong.

"Your Highness, the crown prince isn't aware of your presence. He believes he's being allowed to rest. Of course, as your schedule increases to more public appearances, he will be informed."

"In other words, if Princess Lucille speaks to him, the real crown prince, he won't recall their encounter."

Both of my assistants nodded.

"She needs to be told the truth."

Lord Martin's lips came together, forming a straight line.

Standing from the chair, my volume grew. "She must be told."

"The princess is leaving for Monovia later this evening. There's an excellent probability that she and the crown prince will not see one another much less speak before she leaves."

"They're married," I said emphatically.

"Yes," Lady Caroline replied. "As I was saying, their relationship is strained. After five years of marriage, it was assumed—"

Lord Martin cleared his throat, stopping Lady Caroline's explanation.

My attention turned to him. "If you want me to continue this charade, I must be informed."

Lord Martin nodded to Lady Caroline.

She took a deep breath. "It was assumed that they would have heirs by now. That weighs heavily on your —the prince's mind. He has had Princess Lucille examined by many physicians and specialists. They all say she is capable of conceiving."

"Then it's him," I said.

"The physicians say he is capable," Lord Martin said.

My eyes widened. "I didn't sign up to impregnate the princess."

Both of my assistants shook their heads.

"No, Your Highness," Lord Martin replied. "Of

course not. In all reality, your exposure to the princess is meant to be minimal. There may be public outings. In the future, all personal interactions should be avoided."

"I kissed her," I confessed.

After looking at one another, their stares were back on me.

Pacing to the large windows overlooking the palace grounds, I stopped and stood. I wasn't seeing the vibrant colors of the changing leaves or the pristine gardens. I was seeing Lucille's blue gaze, her cheekbones, and her luscious lips. I was hearing her voice as she endlessly apologized for speaking to the crowd. I'd wanted to tell her that she was marvelous and strong and that her people...*our* people loved her.

"Your Highness, are you listening to me?" Lord Martin asked.

I turned back to him. "No."

He nodded. "Very well. I was saying that what is done is done. We will work diligently to avoid any future interaction with the princess. Will you relay to us what was said to Queen Anne?"

I tried to recall. In the grand scheme of the celebration, the conversation with the queen was mundane. "She asked about the tariffs she said I'd imposed on imports."

"And you said...?" Lord Martin probed.

"I told her not to worry about them, that I had it all handled."

He nodded. "Very good."

"She also mentioned Princess Lucille's" —I took a breath, recalling her wording— "stunt was the word she used."

"The princess spoke to a crowd outside Annabella Castle," Lady Caroline explained.

"I saw it on the telly. She was outstanding."

"You didn't say that to Queen Anne, did you, sir?" she asked.

"I wanted to. I didn't appreciate her calling it a stunt." Both of my listeners were waiting with bated breath. "I told her that I was handling that as well."

Lord Martin and Lady Caroline exhaled.

"Had I?" Before they could respond, I added, "This isn't a matter of state. It is something that as Roman Godfrey's double, I should know."

"Yes, you handled the situation with the princess," Lady Caroline said. "In private, but your displeasure was heard by others."

My stomach twisted. "He shouted?"

They both nodded.

"No wonder she was apologizing," I said, looking back out the window and wondering how anyone could yell at or berate someone as intuitive as the princess. When I turned back, I continued, "I saw the video posted to Twitter. The people of Molave love Princess Lucille. Her promise was reassuring to them. Why would the prince be angry?" Before they could answer, I voiced my next thought. "Because he's always angry."

Lord Martin nodded. "Yes, Your Highness, that is the simple answer."

"Is that why the Firm hired me, to repair his reputation?" And then another thought hit me. "I was told the Firm consisted of the royal family." I shook my head. "Queen Anne didn't know that I wasn't Roman. Does King Theodore know of me?"

"They will be informed once you have perfected the role."

"You're doing splendidly," Lady Caroline added.

"Is this even legal?"

"It is all being handled by the Firm. With King Theodore's age and declining health, the crown prince must mend some international relationships or Molave will find itself on the outside of historically friendly alliances."

I looked from one to the other. "Then work it out with the Firm. If I am to mend alliances, I need more information." This assignment was more like improv than acting. "I must know what has occurred, what requires fixing, and why. Why did the crown prince place tariffs on imports?"

Lord Martin bowed his head and looked back up. "Your Highness, I will implore the chief minister to speak with you directly. She is the one to authorize the sharing of information."

"Then bring her to me—today."

With a slight grin, Lord Martin nodded.

"Your dinner, Your Highness," Lady Caroline said, "will arrive shortly." She lifted the padded shirt. "It would be best for you to appear as him."

"Have that one cleaned. I have another in the bedchamber."

Walking through the apartment toward the bedchamber, I entertained reservations about the reality that I had accepted this position. With each passing day, I contemplated resigning. These weren't my problems. I could leave, go back to the US, and resume my life.

What if I did?

What would happen with Molave?

What about Princess Lucille?

Should I care?

The answer was no, I shouldn't.

I did.

CHAPTER
10

Lucille

I'd forced myself to eat the meal in front of me, each bite more difficult to swallow than the last as the royal family conversed. No one mentioned that Roman seemed odd, nor did they care that he was absent for the meal, especially not with the presence of King Theodore.

I skirted the obligatory questions of my wellness. While Queen Anne was kind, she was asking if I were pregnant. I was most certain that if that were the case, she would be informed before I.

Despite the fact Roman wouldn't approve, a few sips of wine helped the food go down.

Rothy was quite the character. By the time the cake arrived, the young prince was ready for bed. Princess Isabella convinced him to blow out the candles and smile for the camera. It was a lot to ask of a child, in my opinion. As with any other matter, my opinion was not consulted.

"If you'll excuse us," Isabella announced as she

lifted Rothy from his highchair. In seconds, the nanny was at her side helping Alice from her highchair. Before leaving the dining room, Princess Isabella laid her hand on my shoulder. "Could I bother you to help me?"

I blinked as her question registered.

I'd told the people outside Annabella Castle that I'd speak to the king. The problem was I had no idea what to say or anything about the tariffs. Isabella was giving me a chance to learn.

"Yes, of course," I said, standing and placing my napkin on the table near the bottom of my plate. It was the unspoken signal telling the staff that I was done and wouldn't return to eat what remained.

"Lucille," Queen Anne said, "you don't want to miss cake."

The food churned in my stomach. Tucking one foot behind the other, I curtsied. "Your Majesty, I welcome the chance to spend time with Rothy and Alice."

Her smile bloomed. "Isabella is a wonderful mother. She can teach you many things."

"If you will excuse me," I said with a bow to both the king and queen and turned to leave.

"Lucille."

I turned back at the boisterous address from King Theodore. "Your Grace."

His smile dimmed. "I was told you'd be heading back to Monovia tonight."

"Yes."

"What is the rush?"

There wasn't a rush. It was the order of my husband. I wasn't supposed to be here, and he wanted me gone as soon as possible. "I have matters there," I said, hoping my vague answer would be satisfactory.

"I think it would be better if you stayed here at the palace in Molave." His dark eyes were clear as he added, "Would you consider staying on for a few days?"

My cheeks rose as I bowed my head. "Yes, sir. If that is your wish."

"It is."

King Theodore didn't need to ask me to stay. He simply could declare it, and yet he hadn't. Roman shouldn't be upset. Disobeying a direct order from the king would be grounds for reprimand. Staying would mean I obeyed.

By the time I caught up with Princess Isabella, the nanny, and children, they were on their way up the grand staircase. The walls that reached up twenty meters were filled with portraits from generations of the Godfrey monarchy. I stilled on the stairway, my attention on a portrait of King Theodore, Queen Anne, and Roman and Isabella when young.

Roman resembled his father.

Would our son?

Would we have a son?

"Lucille," Isabella called.

"Coming."

The apartments where Isabella and Francis resided in the palace had been refurbished, turning what had been a study into a nursery large enough for both children. There was even a small attached room where the nanny slept.

This wasn't my first time in the nursery, but as I entered, I was struck with the light colors and lack of formality that most of the rooms within the palace contained. Isabella helped Rothy ready for a bath as the nanny placed Alice in a circular contraption that played music as Alice bounced. When the nanny disappeared to draw Prince Rothy's bath, I went to Alice, crouching down and talking to the young child. Her light hair was down to her shoulders, long for her age from what I'd been told.

Her little legs had rolls as she bounced and giggled.

"Do you mind staying with Alice?" Isabella asked. "Once Rothy is bathed, we can speak privately."

"I don't mind at all."

I was not well-versed in young children; however, it was not difficult to sense that as time passed, Alice's discontentment with her surroundings grew. When neither Isabella nor the nanny appeared, I spoke to the infant princess.

"I can pick you up if you'd like."

Her eyes squinted as she fussed.

Lifting her below her arms, I brought her to my shoulder, and she immediately quieted.

With one hand behind her head and the other arm holding her to me, I swayed and sang a song I recalled from my childhood. The words to *Hush, Little Baby* came back without thought as I quietly sang. Alice's posture relaxed as she lay her head on my shoulder.

"You're a natural," Isabella said, coming in behind me.

I spun around with a smile. "She's precious. I don't know how you don't hold her every minute."

"Let me take her."

Nodding, I handed over my niece.

After Alice was lying in the crib, Isabella smiled my direction. "Come to my apartments. Francis will stay downstairs with Papa and Mum and give a moment."

"Rothy?" I asked.

"Lady Sherry will put him to bed. He's exhausted and as you might hear, not exactly princely at the moment."

I grinned. I had heard a few noises from the direction of the bath that didn't sound joyous.

Soon, we were together in the parlor of Isabella and Francis's apartments. As we sat, I had the realization that as was the case at Annabella Castle, Roman's and my private apartments had a shared parlor connecting our bedchambers. The celebratory meal rolled in my stomach.

My old apprehensions were back. Whatever had occurred earlier this evening no longer gave me confidence in our next meeting, the one where I would inform him that I was staying in Molave City, king's orders.

"Wine?" Isabella asked as she poured red wine into a stemmed goblet.

"No." My confrontation with Roman would be precarious enough without him smelling wine on my breath. A woman who was trying to conceive didn't consume alcohol.

Taking her glass, Isabella sat on one of the long sofas. "What does it mean, you've been sheltered?"

"I realized recently that I was not able to access information about Molave. My phone, tablet, and laptop have been restricted."

Isabella's eyes widened. "Why? As a member of the royal family, you must stay informed."

"Only if my assistance or opinion was desired."

"Roman needs to get over himself. He's been making a mess of things, and now with the tariffs, he's upsetting our people. Maybe he wants to protect you."

I looked down at my hands in my lap and back to Isabella. "Thank you for talking to me. No one else is willing to tell me what's happening." I shrugged. "They've probably been forbidden."

She set her glass on the table and leaned forward. "No one has forbidden me nor will they. I've spoken to Mum, but not Papa."

"What has Queen Anne said?"

"The Firm is concerned. Mum thinks Roman is perfectly suited for his current and future role. The remainder of the Firm is less certain."

"And what can they do?" I asked.

"They called him here to Molave City in hopes of curtailing some of his" —she brought her lips together — "his offenses. From what Mum said, Roman has been in long meetings with Mrs. Drake as well as other royal officials and members of Parliament. They're worried that he will say or do something that could jeopardize the country."

I shook my head. "I know nothing of this."

"Surely, Roman explained why he was absent from Annabella Castle."

"We rarely talk."

Isabella's gaze narrowed. "Heirs?"

Inhaling, I spoke truthfully. "We do that. It doesn't require much in the way of conversation."

"If he has harmed you—"

"Sadness," I interrupted, unwilling to share too much. "I want to be more to him and to Molave." I met Isabella's gaze. "King Theodore asked me to stay. Roman thinks I'm leaving tonight."

Isabella shook her head. "With the unrest, it's dangerous for you to travel. Papa asked Francis and I to stay another few days."

A sigh of relief escaped my lips. "That means you'll be here too?"

"For a few days. Francis is satisfied with our guards. He wants to get back to Forthwith."

That was the province in Molave where they lived.

"Forthwith hasn't seen the uprisings that Monovia and the capital have," she said.

"Are they—the Firm—making progress with Roman?"

Isabella shrugged. "You saw him this evening. He's his old grumpy self."

"He seemed different with me."

"Then maybe," she said, "there is progress. If different means better."

I let my smile show. "It was. For only a moment, but it was." The same smile dimmed. "I'm concerned he'll not be pleased that I'm staying in Molave City."

"Then he can take it up with Mum or Papa."

"I will suggest that. What can you tell me about the tariffs?"

"As you know, Molave exports our mined resources and imports most perishable and consumable items."

My months of training on top of what I'd learned over the last five years confirmed what she was saying. "Yes. The tariffs are on imports or exports?"

"Imports, costing the citizens and benefiting the crown."

"Why? Does the crown need the extra funds?"

"Roman believes so. Francis has another theory."

"Which is?" I asked.

"He believes Roman put the tariffs in place in retaliation because of the mining strike."

I shook my head. "I know so little."

Isabella lifted her glass of wine to her lips. "No matter the reason, the taxation is costly, and the citizens aren't accustomed to the additional expense." She looked around. "Mum has taken the customary role of staying away from the workings of the country. I wish Papa were stronger."

The customary role that I was supposed to continue.

"I could be more involved," I said.

"As you should. Molave is ready to move out of the dark ages."

Before I could respond, the main door to the apartments opened. My breath caught as Roman entered, a step behind Francis. My pulse sped up as if I'd been caught in another situation of which he wouldn't approve. Immediately, I stood and curtsied. "Your Highness."

"I told Roman we'd find you here," Francis said, jovial as usual.

Roman's tone was less pleased. "I told the duke he was mistaken. You had left for Monovia or were preparing to leave as planned."

Isabella stood. "Papa instructed her to stay." When Roman's dark gaze stayed on me, Isabella added, "We all want Princess Lucille safe."

"Yes," he said, his penetrating stare never leaving me.

The dryness in my mouth wasn't the same sensation as earlier today. What currently coursed through me was the all-too-familiar dread of my husband's ire.

"Come, Lucille," he commanded. "We will talk."

He will talk.

As I stepped toward Roman, Isabella reached for my hand. "Tomorrow morning after breakfast. If we're both secluded here, I challenge you to pickle ball."

"Yes," I said with a forced smile.

CHAPTER
11

Lucille

Lady Buckingham and Lord Avery were waiting as Roman and I entered the parlor, connecting our two suites. Their appropriate greetings came with a curtsy and a bow. If I'd had any doubt that the uncharacteristic affection earlier in the evening was an anomaly, the walk back to our apartments in silence reminded me of our reality. At no point did my husband attempt to make contact, verbal or physical. No hand in the small of my back. No reaching for my hand. Not even a word.

With my focus on the doorway to the left, the entrance to my private suite, I stilled at Roman's next decree to my mistress and his attendant.

"Leave us."

My gaze met Lady Buckingham's. There was no avoiding whatever was about to happen. I could wish the crown prince into his Jekyll personality, but that wouldn't make it happen.

Entertaining the idea was madness.

Giving my mistress a nod, I waited as Lady Buckingham and Lord Avery retreated into the palace hallways. Once the door was closed, I inhaled, straightened my neck and shoulders, and met Roman's gaze. The dark brown of his orbs muddied as they scanned over me, from my hair to my shoes.

"You were told to return to Monovia," Roman said, finally breaking the silence.

"King Theodore asked me to stay."

Roman's nostrils flared as he pivoted away and back, his hands balled at his sides. This was his prelude to my admonishment. I knew it well. His lecture was only beginning, yet at the moment, my thoughts were on his necktie. I recalled it had been gray earlier this evening, and my eyes were telling me it was blue. The starched white shirt and dark gray suit looked the same. The scent of his cologne was unchanged.

Yet the necktie...

Perhaps I was mistaken about what he'd been wearing earlier.

"Are you listening?" Roman asked, his volume raised.

Tilting my head, I asked, "Did you change your tie?"

"My tie," he repeated, looking down. "Are you mad?"

My gaze met his. "I think I am." I took a step closer

and spoke clearly. "I'm going mad, Roman. I'm imagining things and seeing things."

"You need help."

"I do, from you, from my husband. I meant what I said, I don't know you anymore. Being locked away at Annabella is..." I didn't want to unleash my thoughts on a man who wouldn't care, but in this world, there was no one else. "...maddening. And now I've learned that I've been shielded." I used the word I'd been told. "I am the princess. I need to understand what's happening in our country."

"You have one job."

To produce an heir.

"Then give me more." Before he could reply I went on, "I know you're riled at me. Have you ever considered that I am so thirsty for any attention from you that I'll take the bad if it's my only option?"

It was the most honest I'd been with him in years. I supposed the honesty started this afternoon when I spoke freely.

For a moment, Roman stood dumbfounded, his lips agape, until he straightened his shoulders. "Have I considered...?" His timbre slowed as his volume rose. "No, Lucille. I have more important things to consider than your fragile feelings. You are not special. Everyone has responsibilities."

"Do you care for me at all?"

"Care? Of course, I care. You're my wife."

I lifted my chin. "I'm also your princess."

"Yes."

"What are the important things...the responsibilities that dominate your thoughts?"

With a deep breath, Roman took a step back. Before he spoke, he poured bourbon in a tumbler and sat at the end of one of the long sofas. Unbuttoning his jacket, he leaned back. "Sit."

Obediently, I went to the chair at his side and sat on the edge, my ankles crossed beneath the seat and my hands poised on my lap.

Raking me over with his gaze, he scoffed before taking a healthy drink. "What do you know...about what's happening?"

I swallowed the lump in my throat, the one forming because for the first time, Roman was actually speaking with me, not to me. "I know there's unrest. It's why King Theo asked me as well as Francis and Isabella to stay in Molave City."

"You never should have left Monovia."

Earlier he'd insinuated that subject was closed. Understandably with the change in plans, he could reopen it.

"Was I to go against the king's wishes?"

Roman took another drink and turned my way, his slender lips curling into a grin. There was no happiness in his eyes, giving me a chill and sending goose bumps over my flesh. "Convenient to speak to Papa."

"You didn't stay. He wasn't at the gift ceremony. I think everyone was surprised to see him in the dining room." I smiled. "He looks good." It was only partially true. King Theodore had looked better. Nevertheless, his presence was more than welcomed by everyone.

"Stay?" Roman shook his head. "I've seen him."

"He said to tell you that you were missed."

Another scoff.

"With his striving for perfection and outdated beliefs... He doesn't see..." Roman's head shook as he set the crystal tumbler on the table, more forcefully than necessary and stood. "The physicians believe intrauterine insemination may help."

He is talking about artificial insemination?

"What?" I asked, standing. "I should be consulted on such matters."

"It is your one duty."

Thoughts and questions clouded my thoughts as I sank back to the chair.

Turning my way, Roman reached for the arms of the chair. Gripping each one and caging me in, he leaned over me. The alcohol on his breath created a fog growing denser with each of his words. "I won't allow it."

Good. He was talking about the IUI.

"Thank you."

"You misunderstand me."

Blood drained from my cheeks, settling in my feet and making me feel faint. My mouth was suddenly dry. Despite his closeness and obvious irritation, I didn't falter. "Your Highness?"

"I won't allow you to steal the affection of my citizens and that of my father. A child will but cement—"

"I'm but the moon."

"The moon is silent." His grip of the arms of the chair intensified. "What you do...you make a laughing-stock of me. Is that your intention?"

"No, Your Highness. Tell me what I can do to please you."

"Obey. Stay at Annabella. Do not go out into the provinces."

"And do what?" I questioned.

Roman took a step back, standing tall.

I followed, rising to my feet, meeting him chest to chest. "How may I assist with the unrest? Explain to me why you enacted the tariffs on imports."

"I shall have Lady Buckingham remove all the electronics from your possession."

My rebuttal came before I gave it thought. "No."

Roman's lips quirked. "It is within my power."

"I will not stand for it."

He scoffed. "It would serve you right for the

audacity of your whining. You're talking about things you do not know."

I spoke louder, lifting my hands and allowing them to drop at my sides. "Then explain what I don't understand. Don't leave me in the dark any longer."

"Explain," Roman said. "The ice in Greenland is melting."

His answer surprised me. I tried to make sense of it. "Molave's greenhouse emissions are minor. We have wind and hydro—"

"Yes, we are but a small part. Greenland is rich with resources similar to ours. If those resources are exposed due to the ice melt, Molave's resources will lose value."

"You're concerned about Molave's future because of Greenland?"

"I'm concerned because without the funds generated with our mining, we will be at a disadvantage. Already there are requests for upping our exports at a reduced cost."

"What does King Theo think?"

Roman huffed and turned a circle. "It isn't as simple as I explained. The crown prince of Borinkia, Alek Volkov, and I have been in talks."

"Alek Volkov?" Borinkia was a relatively new country to the east of Molave. It came into being after Letanonia, my mother's place of birth, was occupied.

Since that time, there were no dealings between the two countries. "In talks about what?" When Roman didn't respond, I said, "The tariffs on imports is to counterbalance the possible losses with exports."

Roman nodded.

"The losses will be to the crown."

"Exactly. As is the revenue from the tariffs."

"The crown comes out even or ahead, and our citizens are the ones who pay," I said in way of summary. "King Theo agrees with the tariffs?"

"Enough," Roman roared. "I won't be questioned by my people, my chief minister, and my wife."

My thoughts were swirling with the issues of unrest. "Is this related to the issues with healthcare?" When he didn't respond, I offered. "Maybe if the citizens understood what was happening and why. Maybe if the crown also took a loss."

"Take a loss. You are mad. The Godfrey monarchy has been solvent for generations. It will not lose both money and standing on my watch."

I took a step closer. "Roman, talk to your citizens. Let them know you care. They love King Theodore. They will love you too."

My eyes closed and my hand flew to my cheek as the sting of his slap radiated through me, setting off alarms and synapses until my body trembled.

Roman's voice boomed, the thunder to the lightning of his strike. "It is not your position to instruct me. I instruct you, and you will be gone, back to Monovia, tomorrow."

With my teeth clenched, I stood unmoving. The sound of his shoes upon the marble floor echoed as the scent of bourbon waned. The opening and slamming of a door reverberated through the parlor. When I opened my eyes, Roman was gone.

I wasn't sure where he'd exited, to his suite or out into the palace. More importantly, nor did I care.

Tears trailed down my cheeks and my temples throbbed as I replayed his final decree in my mind.

Gone.

Back to Annabella Castle.

With my back turned to the main door, I heard it open. My body relaxed at the sound of a soft knock. As I turned, I met Lady Buckingham's gaze. Her attention went to my cheek.

"Lucille."

I nodded.

She reached for my hand. "Come into the suite. I'll get you an ice pack while I finish packing."

"We're not leaving." Her eyes opened in question. "King Theodore asked me to stay." I lifted my hand back to my left cheek. "Roman isn't pleased."

"Stay? For how long?"

Roman said morning. I didn't relay that. Instead, I said, "The king didn't offer a timeline."

"Let me get you settled, and I'll call for clothes to be brought from Monovia."

"Is it safe?"

"You will be safe."

"For the people bringing me clothes?" I shook my head as we stepped into the private parlor. "I don't need more clothes if it will put anyone in danger."

Lady Buckingham smiled. "Your Highness, your concern is noted." She pulled back the satin bedcovering. "Rest. I'll get some ice."

CHAPTER 12

Oliver

Lord Martin announced the arrival of the chief minister. "Mrs. Drake is here to see you, Your Highness."

Mrs. Drake curtsied before coming closer.

Nodding to Lord Martin, he retreated, leaving me alone with the woman in charge of my hire. Losing the accent, I spoke, "The curtsy is unnecessary. You know who I am."

"Remain in character, Oliver. If you don't, you could slip up, and there's no margin of error here."

While there was something reassuring about hearing my real name, the seriousness of her tone brought the reason of this visit to mind.

With the accent intact, I took a seat and gestured to the chair before me. "If this is to continue, I'll need access to more state information."

Mrs. Drake took the seat. Her lips remained sealed.

"What is the end game?" I asked.

She inhaled and exhaled. "In a perfect world, you

would continue to fill in for the crown prince and during his time of recuperation he would see the errors of his recent decisions and step back into his role aligning himself with his father's ways."

"How long exactly do you believe that transformation will take?"

"Do you want more money?" she asked.

I shook my head. "No. This isn't about my compensation." I was living in a palace with assistants at my beck and call. My salary was accumulating in offshore accounts until I resumed my real life. "It's about my future, hell, the future of Molave, a country I barely knew existed a little more than a month ago. What if a perfect world doesn't occur?"

"Your Highness?"

Character, fine.

I pressed my lips together as the prince would do. "What if Prince Roman doesn't conform? Isn't that his prerogative as the sovereign ruler?"

"There is much at stake."

"I have been here over a fortnight."

"And I heard that today's exercise went well. I will be giving Lord Martin a schedule with more appearances."

"The queen spoke of unrest."

Mrs. Drake nodded. "You will reassure your people."

"Why did he levy the tariffs?"

"Mr. Honeswell—"

"No," I said loudly as I stood. "You may not tell me to stay in character and then strip me of that character the moment I ask a question."

Mrs. Drake's lips curled. "Yes, you are doing well."

Possessed.

That was an explanation for what was happening. This was *Invasion of the Body Snatchers* in a poor royal adaptation. And somehow, I'd found myself in the leading role.

"Surely, you don't expect me to undo what the true prince has done."

Mrs. Drake stood. "In a perfect world, he would be the one to do that. However, if that perfect world doesn't exist, then yes, it would be up to you."

"Nothing you're proposing is up to me. You want me to do your bidding."

"You are being compensated to play a role. You, sir, are not writing the script. The Firm is first and foremost interested in Molave and the royal family. This is an unusual situation, but we believe it will work."

I shook my head. "I was informed that the royal family is the Firm. From where I'm standing, I would disagree."

"And why is that, Mr." —she nodded— "Your Highness?"

"Because it seems as though you and I are working independently of the king and queen. I'm concerned that what you've asked me to do is illegal."

"Nothing is illegal when you dictate the laws of the land."

"Molave has a parliament," I reminded her.

"And the king is the parliamentarian. The current king is competent, the future one...I have my concerns. If Roman's plans that put the country at risk become known, he will be forced to abdicate."

"Will he do that?"

"You will in his stead."

I shook my head. "That can't be legal."

"Again, stop thinking as an American. Here the king makes the rules."

"What would happen if Roman abdicated?"

"After King Theodore's passing, Princess Isabella would become queen."

My thoughts were spinning. "She is married to the Duke of Wilmington."

"Of course, he would need to renounce his title."

"You are making many assumptions, Mrs. Drake."

"No, sir. I'm holding the deck of cards in my hands, and I know which card to play."

Shaking my head, I walked to the windows. Darkness veiled the landscape as a light rain pelted the glass. Molavian weather was unlike Southern

California. Cold and damp instead of warm and sunny.

"Your Highness," she said, "leave the crown prince to me. Molave will forever be in your debt."

I spun toward her. "I believe I will be resigning."

Her eyes opened wide. "Roman is paranoid about the crown losing money on our mining." Elizabeth Drake was speaking fast. "Since Borinkia was claimed as a sovereign state ousting the Letanonia regime, Molave has not worked with Borinkia. If Roman Godfrey has his way, the two countries will become one. He believes Molave has the means to take over Borinkia, not through force but through financial occupation. That is one of the reason he's assessed tariffs on imports. Alek Volkov, the prince of Borinkia is using the prince's arrogance as a tool to manipulate him. Roman Godfrey's plans would mean the end of Molave. I implore you, sir, you and only you can save us."

I was an actor, not a politician.

This was life-and-death shit, and I was in the center.

"Who knows what you just told me?"

"I do, my top advisors, as well as a select few in Parliament."

"Who knows I'm an impostor?"

"Mr. Briggs, Lord Martin, Lady Caroline, and myself."

She didn't mention my voice instructor, and I wasn't about to remind her. "The king?" I asked.

"He will."

"If I fail..."

Mrs. Drake shook her head. "You cannot. If my plan doesn't work, Molave will cease to exist."

"You said yourself that the king makes the laws in Molave. If King Theodore would perish, Roman would take the title. He may do as he pleases."

"That is why we must stop him before he takes the crown."

This was ludicrous.

"I can follow a script," I said, "but what you're asking of me requires more than a script. I need to have knowledge, to know what Roman knows. Without that information, I could make a mistake that would have devastating consequences."

Mrs. Drake inhaled and nodded.

"Bring me everything," I said.

"It is classified."

"I am the prince."

She stood tall. "Molave will need your vow."

"You will have it."

She nodded. "Your Highness."

Mrs. Drake left after promising me that the information I requested would come in the morning. There would be more studying. In essence I would need to learn in a matter of weeks what Roman Godfrey acquired through four decades of life.

My head ached.

"Your Highness," Lord Martin said. "Shall I prepare the bedchamber?"

"I need to get out of this apartment."

"It is best..."

"Help me, man," I implored. "An hour outside." I turned toward the windows. "It's cold and rainy. No one else in their right mind will be out. I just need to breathe."

Lord Martin nodded. "I know of a place."

"Thank you."

CHAPTER
13

Lucille

My eyes opened to the dim glow of the nightlight radiating from the bathroom. For a moment, I sat straight, wondering if I'd heard something, and stared into the corners of the bedchamber. The shadows lurked unmoving, nothing but darkness covering the fringe of the room. The tall windows were covered with heavy drapes.

Blinking in the dark, I found my eyes scratchy and my temples throbbing from the tears I'd mostly held at bay. When I first moved to Molave, I was taught the history of the palace. I'd learned the names of duchesses and princesses who had slept in this same suite. I knew their names, dates of birth, and dates of death. I'd studied their portraits, and yet I'd never known about them, their thoughts, hopes, and dreams. I didn't know if they were content or melancholy or if they had ambitions.

As I lay back on the soft pillow recalling my last

row with the prince, I found myself curious as to the novelty of my plight.

Could it be that others were unhappy as I have been?

Was I not special as Roman had said?

Was I ordinary?

The world saw me as a princess living a fairy tale with a charming prince. That was the reflection we portrayed, not the reality.

The tips of my fingers went to my left cheek. While the flesh was tender to the touch, the ice pack had stopped the contusion from swelling, hopefully avoiding much in the way of discoloration. No one would know. Lady Buckingham was a wizard when it came to concealers.

Part of me wanted everyone to know, to walk into the dining room tomorrow morning as I was now, without makeup, to look the king and queen in the eyes, and show them the way I was treated by their son.

And what?

Did I want them to intervene?

I didn't.

I wanted *me* to intervene, and with each tick of the clock, each chime for the hour, and each page of the calendar, I was less competent to stand up to the man I married or perhaps less willing—it was the definition of insanity to do the same thing over and over and expect a different result. If I was incapable of intervening, then maybe it could be Roman's doing. If only he would see me, not as someone who would dare to make him look or feel inferior, but as his mate.

Helper.

Partner.

Our relationship wasn't always as it was now. There was a time I was attracted to him, smitten by him, and perhaps even cared for in his presence. There had been joy in our interactions, a delight when our gazes met, and anticipation of our unions.

The current reality was a sucker punch to the stomach.

Roman wanted me gone.

The seclusion of Annabella Castle was truly wearing on my sanity.

I thought about my parents. It had been over a year since I'd visited the United States. If my husband wanted me gone, I would inquire about a holiday with my family. Yes. That was my plan.

My mind filled with the possibilities in New York.

I imagined donning a Yankees hat and sunglasses, and walking along Fifth Avenue as if I wasn't the Princess of Molave, but simply an ordinary woman. My heart and soul soared as I thought about visiting the Met or strolling in Central Park. While there was nothing I couldn't afford in the high-end stores, there was nothing I wanted or needed.

Nothing material.

Those everyday occurrences of my youth were unappreciated until they were gone. A trip to the US, even to my parents' home, would require an entourage. Lady Buckingham would be at my side nearly every minute. I'd given away more than my last name when I agreed to marry Roman Godfrey. I'd signed away my freedom to be a real person.

Giving up on sleep, I threw back the covers and went to the cupboard. Wearing only a nightgown, I selected a long satin dressing gown and wrapped it around me. The walls of the bedchamber were closing in, and I needed a moment, just a moment truly to myself.

Before Roman and I married, I was housed in a different area of the palace, apartments in another wing. That was where I studied and stayed. At the time, I was enthralled with the attention and eager to learn. I'd always been willing to glean knowledge. That was what was infuriating about my situation. If only Roman would see that I could be an asset.

Jealous.

That was what Isabella said.

Pushing away the memories of the horrible things Roman said, I stepped into the parlor connecting our suites. My gaze went to the doors leading to Roman's side. They were closed tight. With the lateness of the hour, I could assume he was inside. With a chill skirting my skin, I wrapped my arms around my torso.

Roman hadn't called for me.

There was a time when he would at least try to make up for his actions. My empty stomach twisted with the realization that that time had passed. I shouldn't leave the apartments without makeup or wearing nightclothes. My hope was that I wouldn't run into anyone royal. No staff member would dare discuss the princess taking a night stroll.

Opening the door to the hallway, I peered right and left.

The passageway was empty of people.

There were no assistants, secretaries, or guards.

The direction of Francis and Isabella's apartments was equally as quiet. The king and queen's apartments were down another hallway. My bare feet padded along the long rugs as I made my way down a back staircase. My destination was the gardens.

It was where I would go during those first few months.

Nestled safely within the walls of the palace, the gardens were a retreat of sorts, a place where I could feel the cool breeze against my skin and see the stars overhead. Along the paths created with stone slates, I could wander to my heart's content.

I was no longer naïve enough to believe I would find contentment. I was perhaps searching for a moment beneath the large sky to remember that I was but one person, not a princess or queen to be, but a single soul in need of a change of scenery.

My hopes dashed as I came to the tall French doors off one of the parlors. The panes were sprinkled with water droplets and the pathway was wet.

How had I not bothered to even peer beyond the window?

I recalled an old stone gazebo near the far end of the gardens. I'd been told that King Theodore wanted it removed, but Queen Anne insisted it stay. The structure dated back centuries older than the palace itself. If I hurried through the drizzle, I could make it to the shelter of the gazebo.

Stepping outside as the rain coated my hair and my bare feet chilled on the wet pavement, I determined that what I'd told Roman was true. I was officially mad —a head case. No sane person would leave the warmth and security of her bedchamber in the middle of the night to see stars that were obscured by rain clouds and still, when met with a reason to turn around, persist.

With my head down, I hurried along the paths. In the cooler temperature, my exhales were visible in puffs of clouds. Puddles splashed my feet and ankles. There was no doubt Lady Buckingham would see the hem of the dressing gown and know what I had done. She wouldn't be upset, only caution me against wandering on my own.

I was rarely on my own.

That fact alone invigorated me as I neared the gazebo.

By the time I caught sight of the structure, I was chilled and out of breath. Although my body trembled from the cold, my thinking was clearer than it had been in weeks. The chill was invigorating. Running through the pathways where I used to roam was exhilarating. If I were in a real-life fairy tale, I might break into a song. While I knew life wasn't a fairy tale, this mini-escape gave me a strange sense of freedom that I wanted to savor.

Dashing up the steps of the gazebo, I came to a sudden stop.

The bubble I'd created popped as Roman turned his body toward me. His eyes widened with surprise. My heart was thumping so loudly I was sure he could hear it.

"Your Highness," I said through shivers as I curtsied.

CHAPTER
14

Lucille

L ooking up, I panicked, my explanation coming too fast. "I'm sorry. I didn't realize. I thought I might take a moment." I bowed my head. "I'll go back."

"Why do you always apologize?"

I looked up, staring at the man before me.

My cooled fingers came to my lips as I tried to make sense out of what was happening. I finally managed to speak. "Your accent is gone." I took a step closer. "Who are you?"

This made no sense and at the same time, it made all the sense.

Wrapping my arms around myself, I backed away, step by step, until I collided with the gazebo's railing. The entire time I shook my head as I felt myself falling through the looking glass.

I wasn't mad.

I wasn't losing my mind.

I'd thought Roman was different earlier this

evening, but never would I nor could I imagine that he was truly a different person. Now, I saw it. In the dark with rain dripping from my hair, I saw what made no sense. This man wasn't Roman Godfrey.

"I-I..."

He reached for my arm. "Please."

Snatching my arm away, I asked, "Who are you?"

"Don't tell anyone you saw me."

"How are you here?" My thoughts scattered in every direction. "How long have you been here? It was you this afternoon. When else have you pretended? Why are you...? Is Roman in danger?"

"You're shivering," he said with Roman's voice, the accent having returned. He looked down, seeing my toes peek out from under the dressing gown. "You must be chilled." He tugged his suitcoat from his shoulders and wrapped it around me.

As the warmth from his body heated my skin, the familiar scent of his cologne filled my senses. Yet as I stared, I knew this wasn't the man I married. "I-I'll call the guards."

"No guards are near." He lifted his chin toward the wing of the palace from which I'd come. "The royal family members are all asleep." He scoffed. "Except you." He tilted his head to the side. "Are you like me?"

"Sir, I don't know who you are." I pulled his large

jacket closed in front of me, covering my intimate apparel. "Explain yourself."

His smile formed without effort in a way I'd longed to see from this man's double.

The man bowed at his waist. "Princess Lucille, it is an honor to be in your presence again."

"It was *you* this afternoon."

"Yes." His dark eyes glistened as the rain continued to fall around us. "I apologize for overstepping my bounds. You and I are not to have contact. When I saw you there, in the dining room, I was besieged with memories. Kissing you was wrong."

"What is your name?"

"If you don't know, you can answer honestly when you report me to the prince."

"He doesn't know about you?"

The man shook his head. "I've been told no."

"Are you here to hurt him?"

"No," he replied. "I was hired to help Molave, due to my" —he waved his hand over his body— "likeness."

There was every reason I should run and scream. And no reason why I should believe or trust a word from this impostor, yet I didn't run. I didn't scream. Under the weight of his jacket and within a cloud of his cologne, I felt strangely secure. I looked to the cement bench in the center of the old gazebo, farthest point from the rain.

"May we sit?" I asked. "My feet..." I grinned. "I should have worn shoes."

"Princess, you don't know me. You should go back to your apartment. It's not right for you to be out here with a strange man."

Sitting, I lifted my feet and tucked them beneath me. Admittedly, the stone bench wasn't comfortable, but the position brought circulation back to my cold toes. I patted the bench at my side. "Please."

The man nodded as he took the seat beside me. "I've been out here for a few hours," he volunteered. "I believe I've decided to return to America."

"Who hired you?" I asked.

"I will be gone tomorrow. The less you know..."

My head shook. "No, sir. There is unrest outside these walls. Whoever you are, you look too much like the prince. You might not be safe. You can't leave."

His smile waned as he gently reached for my chin and turned my face. I'd forgotten about my cheek until now. My chin dropped to my chest, freeing me from his hold. "Please don't ask."

Even in the darkness, I saw the way his jaw clenched.

His voice was Roman's but steadier. "I've spent nearly the last month studying your husband." His nostrils flared. "My disgust of the man grows by the day."

"He can be good," I said.

"You're not convincing, Princess."

A grin lifted my cheeks. "What are you going to do, impostor, tell on me?"

"Never."

I pulled his jacket around me tighter. "I thought I was going mad."

"Why would you think that?"

"I thought I imagined you into existence before the birthday celebration. For a moment in time, you behaved as I have dreamed a husband would."

"The crown prince is a fool if he doesn't cherish you." His head tilted again.

The tilting wasn't something Roman did, and I found the habit fascinating.

"Your cheek," he said.

"I asked you not to speak of it."

"You asked me not to *ask*."

I nodded.

"I wonder if that is why you are always apologizing."

"I'm not," I said defensively.

"I surmise you are like me."

"I'm not an impostor."

"No. That isn't what I meant." He looked out to the rain-soaked gardens. "You needed a break from in there." He tilted his chin toward the palace. "You were looking for an escape."

"I'm not like you, sir. You say you're leaving for America tomorrow. I cannot leave. I'm not an impostor. I'm a prisoner." I wasn't certain of the reason I was speaking so freely. Perhaps it was the realization that my secrets were safer with a stranger than with family. "When the unrest eases to the king's satisfaction, he'll allow me to return to Monovia where I'll stay until the time comes when my husband wants to see me...if the time comes."

"You're an American," he said, still speaking with the accent. "Go home."

I lifted my chin. "This is my home. I made a commitment to Roman, the crown, and Molave. It is not in me to break it."

"I had you pegged wrong."

"Was that before or after you kissed me?"

"Before." His dark eyes sparkled as his smile grew. "I saw you and the crown prince on the telly. You were at an event in London with the Prince and Princess of Wales."

I nodded, recalling that day and night.

"I thought the four of you were ridiculous. I thought monarchs died in the true sense of the word and in political structure centuries ago. I thought the lot of you were playing dress-up and spending your country's wealth."

"You weren't wrong. It is dress-up, pretending, and acting. Nothing is as it appears. Reflections deceive."

"And yet you won't leave?"

I stared out at the rain. "Something is happening with Molave. I don't completely understand Roman's reasoning, but he has levied tariffs, and the people are upset. King Theodore hasn't been able...Roman is perplexed..." I inhaled. "...I want to help."

The man reached over to my hands clenched on my lap. His one hand covered both of mine with warmth. I looked up to rebuke him. Before I could speak, he did.

"I saw the video of you outside Annabella Castle."

My chin dropped.

"No, Princess, you were marvelous. The people, they listen to you. This isn't dress-up or pretend. It's odd and different, but it's a real life, a real country with real people."

I swallowed a lump forming in my throat. "I wish..." I looked down at his hand covering mine and back to his dark gaze. "I wish you were real. As I said, I thought I wished you into being this evening."

The rain continued to fall as we sat staring at one another. His dark gaze was very similar to Roman's, so much so, I could forget this wasn't the man I married. I could get lost in the way he looked at me, really looked. Not only that, but he was also listening, and his touch was warm and comforting. I was about to turn away when his gaze moved to my lips. It was the same look I'd seen this afternoon.

My pulse kicked up and my breaths came quicker.

Small clouds of condensation grew between us.

This was wrong and my mind knew it. I could no longer claim innocence. I knew this man wasn't my husband, and I still wanted him to kiss me as he had. I wanted to find out if I would react the same way now that I knew the truth. I wanted to feel the way I felt one more time before he left for America.

I closed my eyes as I leaned closer.

His warmth pulled me into his orbit—a sun's gravitational pull.

"I shouldn't kiss you," he murmured.

I opened my eyes. "No," I said, shaking my head. "You shouldn't."

And still we moved nearer until our lips met.

Our contact was more tentative than the first time we'd kissed. Yet the give-and-take was still present, as was the way my body reacted. I pressed closer, savoring the union.

Finally, my better sense prevailed. "This is wrong," I said, pulling back a millimeter as warmth filled my cheeks.

Our noses were close enough to touch one another's. No longer was I cool as a new warmth circulated through me, radiating from my head to my toes.

"If you were my wife, Lucille, I would do everything in my power to share moments like this one." He cupped my cheek. "You are so much more than anyone seems to know."

Inhaling, I scooted away. "I think I did create you. And I'm all right with that. I'll keep you to myself." I recalled something he'd said earlier. "You said you kissed me—before—because of memories. What memories?"

The man sat taller. "I told you I've been studying Roman. I've spent hours rehearsing his accent in English and Norwegian."

"I haven't perfected Norwegian," I admitted.

He then said something I didn't understand.

"What does that mean?" I asked.

"I can't tell you."

"You don't know what you said?"

His smile grew. "I know what I said. If I was overheard translating it, Roman would probably have me beheaded."

More warmth came to my cheeks. "No one beheads anymore."

"Firing squad?"

I shook my head.

126

"That is fortunate." He took a breath. "I've been working to copy his mannerisms, dialect, behaviors."

"No one else knew at the celebration," I said, "that you were you or you weren't him."

His eyes dimmed. "I've watched hours and hours of videos from the palace photographers."

"How would you get access to those?"

Instead of answering, he continued his explanation. "I found myself not watching Roman but instead watching you. I wanted to reach into the videos and shake the prince."

"Why? Whatever for?"

Again, his hand covered mine. "Because he has the most sensational woman at his side, and I've had a continuing and overwhelming suspicion that he doesn't appreciate her. When I saw you in the dining room, and you assumed I was the prince, I think I wanted to give you what he should."

"How do you see that void," I asked, "and he doesn't?"

"There are many questions I have about your husband and few answers."

"Is that why you're leaving?"

"Yes and no."

I waited for more.

"Impersonating a royal is not the everyday acting job."

I grinned. "Is that what you are...an actor?"

"Aren't we all?"

"Sadly, yes."

"Tomorrow, I'm supposed to be given top clearance to learn more about the mining demands, tariffs, Borinkia, and more."

I took a quick breath. "What about Borinkia?"

"It isn't for me to share."

I wanted to tell this man I was the princess, but that was redundant. Instead, I said, "Tomorrow, but instead of getting that information you are going to leave?"

"Once I have that information, I'm no longer just an impostor. Molave won't allow me to go back to my life. I haven't been told that, but I know it in my gut. Once I agree to the next level, I'm stuck."

With my lips together, I nodded. "I don't know what agreement you have or with whom, but from experience, I have to agree." I stood and handed him back his jacket. Immediately, my flesh covered with goose bumps and my nipples tightened. Crossing my arms over my breasts, I smiled. "You will stay my secret."

"If you are asked?"

"No one will ask. You see, I'm nothing more than an accessory to be brought out on trips and paraded around. I'm hoping to visit America and my parents soon."

The man stood. "Maybe we could see one another..."

The shaking of my head stopped his sentence.

I pushed up on my tiptoes and brushed his lips with mine. "Goodbye, Your Highness. Thank you for fulfilling my wish for one night."

He reached for my hand.

When I turned back, he was down on one knee.

"What?" I asked.

Still holding my hand, he forced a smile. "I'm learning the rules. From what I've been told, as prince I only bow to the king and queen. Princess Lucille, know that I will always bow to you."

His lips brushed my knuckles seconds before I pulled away, running down the stairs, into the rain, and through the paths. By the time I reached the French doors I was frigid, soaked, and trembling.

Leaving a trail of wet footprints, I made my way back up to our private apartments, slipped into my suite, then into my bedchamber, and stripped off my wet clothes before filling the tub with warm water.

As I sank into the bath and submerged my hair, I grinned.

"Thank you, impostor," I murmured. "Stay safe."

CHAPTER 15

Oliver

Lord Martin sprang from the chair where he'd been waiting as I entered the apartment. "Your Highness," he said with a bow. Rushing toward me, he reached for my wet suit coat. "We can't have you getting ill."

"I'm well."

The rain dripped from the suit coat in his hand. "I was worried. You were gone longer than I expected. Were you seen? Did you need to convince anyone that you were the prince?"

"I didn't convince anyone." That was the truth. I'd been completely honest. Seeing Lord Martin's concern, I continued, "It's frigid, cold, and the middle of the night. I found the gazebo. You were right. The gardens were a perfect place to think."

"Very well," he said, taking each of my wrists and removing the jeweled cufflinks. Next, he began to unbutton my shirt. "I hope the padded shirt isn't wet. The other one is being cleaned..."

As Lord Martin went on talking about my wetness and clothes, my mind was on Princess Lucille. She'd said she conjured me from her imagination. The truth was that I couldn't possibly conjure her in mine. If I did, I'd never do her justice.

Soaked to the skin, Lucille was beyond beautiful. I marveled at her sincerity for Molave and her welcoming manner. At the same time, it concerned me that she would trust a man she didn't know as she had me.

What if I had meant her harm?

I didn't want to think about the slight abrasion on her cheek. Yet I couldn't stop. After all, seeing it was part of the reason for my new decision.

"I'll draw your bath, Your Highness. It will warm you before bed. Would you like some hot tea?"

"Does the prince ever partake of spirits stronger than wine?"

"Why, yes," he said with a smile. "Bourbon."

"A double. It will warm me fine. I'll bathe first thing in the morning." I would rather shower. Apparently, that wasn't a thing. The palace had showers, but the royal family bathed.

Lord Martin clutched his hands behind his back. "If I may?"

My shoulders slumped and my head fell to the side. "For the love of all things holy, you may."

"Very well," he said with a grin. "I was worried about you stepping out, but you seem lighter, better. I understand that portraying the crown prince is exhausting."

"It is a drudgery. If *I* may, he's a childish, boorish, pompous ass."

Lord Martin's smile dimmed. "Have you changed your mind? Will you be leaving us?"

That was my plan.

I had the reservations set in my mind. Images of my apartment and my cactus were running through my thoughts. The warm sunshine and the nearby beach were all beckoning me home.

Until...

"Tomorrow," I said, "Mrs. Drake will deliver information necessary for me to take this to the next level."

"Yes." He stammered.

"You may," I encouraged.

"Once you learn what it is you need to learn..."

"There's no turning back. I came to that revelation tonight."

"And still, you're not leaving?"

"I'm not." I repeated part of what Lucille said earlier. "I will commit to Molave and the crown." And to the princess.

Lord Martin beamed. "Bravo, Your Highness. Molave thanks you."

"As long as Molave doesn't behead me."

"No, sir. We imprison."

"That's what I heard."

I'm not an impostor. I'm a prisoner. The princess's words rang true.

"I'll get your bedclothes ready."

"Lord Martin" —I paused— "tomorrow I will make that vow. Tonight, I will put on my own pajamas."

He grinned. "Yes, Your Highness."

"I will also take that double."

Once I was alone with my double neat, I stepped into the bedchamber. My covers were turned down and satin pajamas with the Godfrey crest were laid on the bed. Taking a hefty drink, I felt the familiar burning. As I looked around, I questioned my own sanity.

I'd told Lord Martin that no one in their right mind would be out on a night like tonight. Lucille confessed she'd been afraid she was going mad. Maybe we were both insane. There was no other explanation for what she had done and what I was about to do.

We didn't owe anything to Molave. There was no birthright for either of us. We were foreigners in a country that was stuck in the past, mired in the muck of centuries of traditions and rituals. And yet Molave was also a new and modern country. It had cell service, advanced Wi-Fi, a state-of-the-art infrastructure, and was one of the world's largest sources of titanium and rhodium.

The citizens consisted of two classes. There was the top percent who owned land and businesses and benefited from the natural resources. And there was the majority, those who kept the sovereign state running. They mined, worked in the shipyards, cleaned the streets, served the people in the restaurants and stores, and willingly worked from sunup to sundown to reside in a country that supported them and kept them safe.

The citizens of Molave have been content for centuries until recently.

Was that why I would take a vow to this country?

No.

If there was a way for me to make a difference on an international front, I would. I would also make a difference on the home front. Once I was in a position to make declarations, Princess Lucille's days of isolation at Annabella Castle would end.

If memory served me, I recalled reading that she'd graduated from Columbia University. Lucille wasn't an accessory to be paraded about. If it took an impostor to give her voice, then so be it. I would be that impostor.

"The hell with tradition," I murmured as I eyed the rarely used shower.

One more night.

With bourbon coursing through me, I turned on the spray and waited for it to heat.

Tonight, I was Oliver.

Tomorrow, I would take the leap and commit to Molave, the citizens, and their princess.

* * *

The next morning after breakfast, Mrs. Drake arrived with buggies filled with boxes.

"Does Molave not understand that all of this" —I pointed— "can be put on a flash drive?"

"No, Your Highness, it can't. Once you commit to the state, you will bear witness to documents that will never be put on a computer. They are far too sensitive, too classified, and too important to risk that any of this information could end up in the wrong hands."

Dressed in character, I nodded. "I have a lot to learn, Mrs. Drake."

"Yes, you do."

The boxes were taken to the study, a room in the apartment.

"Do you have any guidance on where to start?" I asked as the boxes were unloaded by rather scary-looking men not dressed in royal uniforms.

"First, I need your signature confirming your commitment."

I looked down at the document. "And what name do I sign?"

"Your Highness, from this moment on, there is only one name that you will sign."

Gripping the pen, I scrolled *Roman Archibald Godfrey*. I'd been practicing his penmanship as well.

"Let us begin," she said.

For the next hour, the chief minister worked with me, starting my education many centuries before I thought necessary.

"You must know the past to understand the present," she admonished. "I wouldn't have gathered these documents for you if they weren't important."

"Well then, I shall continue."

The chief minister nodded toward the door. "There will always be a deputy of the ministry with these records. Once your day is complete, the guard will lock the door to your study. In the morning, it will be opened. You may not take even one document out of this room."

Nodding, I took it all in. "I understand, Mrs. Drake."

"There is one more thing."

I looked up from the stacks of papers. "What is it?"

"King Theodore requests an audience with you."

CHAPTER
16

Lucille

With each passing day, I wondered what became of the impostor. I assumed he'd returned to America. After all, that was what he'd said he would do. It wasn't as if I could ask. I didn't know who was privy to his presence. In some strange way, our night and talk helped me. Lady Buckingham even remarked about a change in me.

During the first week of my stay in Molave City, each morning, weather permitting, Isabella and I met out at the pickle ball court. As we played, I realized I was having fun. I wasn't lamenting about my husband or the lack of his attention. Since our quarrel, the only time we'd been in the same room was for evening dinner with the rest of the family. We played our roles for the observers. In private, we rarely saw one another and when we did, we didn't speak. I didn't feel the need to push for his attention.

After an evening with the impostor, it wasn't Roman's attention I wanted.

No longer did the role of princess seem like drudgery. I now thought of it as acting, as the impostor had referred to it. Each day and activity were a game I played with myself. The reflection in the mirror was of Molave's princess. The young woman drinking tea with the queen was who I strove to be. Understanding that it was all make-believe eased the pressure.

Of course, I was careful in the prince's presence to keep my newfound contentment hidden. I could never explain that for one conversation in the dark of night, soaked to the skin, I had the husband I'd dreamed of. I couldn't tell anyone that my memories of that night would sustain me.

I wasn't certain they would—at least not how long they would.

For now, I was content.

While the Duke and Duchess of Wilmington were still in Molave City, after tea, I would go with Isabella to the children. Their sweet laughter reminded me what it was like to live without the veil of pretentiousness. While Isabella tried to instill princely behavior into Prince Rothy, it was quickly forgotten. Princess Alice was too young to understand what would one day be expected of her.

While my electronics were still shielded within Molave Palace, I counted it as a win that I still had them. Until Isabella and her family went back to

Forthwith, Isabella was my source of information. Over that first week the unrest calmed. The news made me both happy and sad. I was happy for the citizens and melancholy for myself. Safety would mean that soon I would be sent back to Monovia to Annabella Castle.

Despite the princess and her family leaving, over two weeks after arriving, I was still in the capital, Molave City.

Dressed for dinner, I stood at the window in my parlor, looking out to the front of the palace. The tempered glass shielded me from the people below. The scene was back to normal, much as I recalled it being for most of the five and a half years I'd lived in Molave. Citizens walked by. Tourists took photos. The agitation was gone. I didn't need Isabella to tell me. I could see it for myself.

Turning to the sound of the opening door, I expected Lady Buckingham. Instead, I was met with my husband's dark stare.

"Your Highness," I said with a curtsy.

Roman was dressed for dinner in his customary suit paired with a silver necktie. I found it amusing that I noticed each color of his ties. Coldness rolled off him, much like the chill from a frozen tundra. With no emotion in his expression, he announced, "I spoke with Papa."

I nodded my understanding. Roman didn't need to say more. "I will be going back to Monovia."

"Tonight," he said, coming closer.

Tonight?

My chin fell. That was so soon.

My breathing hitched as Roman reached for my chin, lifting my gaze to his. "Something is different about you." His touch disappeared.

"No, Your Highness. I am the same."

"Lady Buckingham tells me you've been eating better."

"Why would she report to you?"

"I inquired."

"While the duke and duchess were here, I enjoyed spending time with Isabella, Rothy, and Alice."

Taking a deep breath, Roman turned toward the window. "Mum told me that you want to travel to the States." He turned back to me. "Why wouldn't I hear that directly from you?"

Because we don't speak.

An apology was on the tip of my tongue when I recalled the impostor's question. Instead of apologizing, I stood tall with my shoulders back. "I have daily afternoon tea with the queen. You and I don't speak."

Roman's neck straightened as he clasped his hands behind his back. "My suite is across the parlor, mere meters away. If you want to speak, come speak."

I blinked, wondering if by chance this wasn't my husband. "Your Highness?"

"I've told you before that I have other priorities."

My fleeting hope disappeared. This was Roman Godfrey. The impostor was gone.

He went on, "If you have matters to discuss, have the initiative to bring them to me."

"I would like to plan a trip to visit New York."

"The family feels it would be better if we traveled together and visit more cities than New York."

My heart sank. He knew what I wanted and was ready to change it.

A tour.

I didn't want a tour. I wanted time to see my family.

"And your thoughts?" I asked. When he didn't reply, I added, "You said the family feels... What are your feelings, Roman?"

"After the holidays."

"It is October."

Roman scoffed. "Always so smart."

My teeth came together as I stared. "It has been over a year since I've seen my parents."

"They may come to Annabella."

I nodded. "I will ask."

I would.

They wouldn't. Not because they wouldn't want to

visit. I knew this was a busy time of year for them both. The Senate was soon in session, and my mother's schedule always picked up this time of year. Curtsying, I added, "I will inform Lady Buckingham of our scheduled departure."

"Shall we go downstairs?"

For a moment, I hoped for his arm, the simple gesture the impostor had made. There wasn't such a gesture or any form of touch. Roman turned and walked toward the door. Watching the back of his head and shoulders, each step he took infuriated me more than the last.

"I'm not a dog," I called out.

When he turned back, his expression was perplexed. "You are mad."

"Mad as in angry." My volume was raised. "You expect me to follow. You call and I should heel. I am your wife. I should be next to you, not two paces behind."

"Where is this coming from?"

I shook my head, unwilling to devote more energy to what was irrevocably dead. "Forget it, Roman. Give your family an excuse. Lady Buckingham and I will pack my things, and we will be gone before you return from dinner."

"Absolutely not. You will eat."

"I'm not hungry."

"Your duty—"

"I've been doing my duty," I interrupted. "Not that you notice anything I do."

Roman charged my direction, stopping millimeters away. His tone was harsh. "Maybe you should notice all that I do." Yet the characteristic reddening of his neck and face were absent.

I stood my ground. "I don't see you."

He shook his head. "Go to Annabella. I'll tell Papa and Mum you couldn't wait to get out of here and back to Monovia. I'll tell them that you have little respect for the monarchy. You're much more concerned about sulking where no one can see."

"I respect them."

"What about me?" His timbre slowed.

"I respect you. Do you respect me?"

To my complete shock, Roman fell to one knee.

"Princess Lucille, so much so, I chose to stay."

Tears filled my eyes, and my fingertips flew to my lips as I tried to swallow. "You're...I believed..."

My impostor stood. "I've been working diligently. I believed if I could fool you..."

I reached up to his cheek with my trembling palm as I stared into his eyes. "How do you do it? You're so realistic. And the things you said..."

He took my hand in his. "I hated most of it. Truth be told, I hate most of what he says. I was told you wouldn't protest the decision regarding the States."

Gazing down at where we were touching, I savored the warmth of his hand holding mine. When I looked up, I marveled at the likeness while relishing the presence of this other man. "I wouldn't have," I confessed, "before you."

"Me?"

"I've relived our night, our conversation, in my thoughts over and over." I shook my head. "Where is Roman?"

"I haven't been told."

"How long..." I had so many questions. "...when did you step in?"

"Yesterday morning."

I tried to recall. "I was told you were with King Theo yesterday."

He nodded.

My eyes opened wide. "Does he know?"

"He does. He accepted my vow."

"Your vow? Why would you give him that?"

This man was still holding my hand. "Because, Princess, without it, I couldn't continue."

"No. You were going to escape. You should be back in America."

He lifted my hand to his lips. "I've been told we don't do this."

"This?"

His voice was Roman's, but the timbre was slower, more confident, and his earlier cold expression was gone. The one before me was animated and looking right at me.

"Talk," he said. "Connect."

Warmth filled my cheeks. "We don't."

"Princess Lucille, I need your assistance to succeed."

I swallowed. "You're sending me back to Monovia."

He nodded. "Because that's what Roman would do. And..."

"And?" I prompted.

His next phrase was in Norwegian. I recognized the language, not the words.

"Your Highness?" I questioned.

"I'm not to be trusted with you."

"Did the king—?"

"No, I know you're not my wife. The problem is that if I'm to become Roman Archibald Godfrey in all senses, I want every part of his life, including you. That can never be."

I nodded.

He was right. We couldn't, and at the same time, he wanted me. This man I barely knew wanted me. I was wanted. My heart didn't seem to mind that this man was an impostor. It was too busy soaring.

"He will be back," the impostor said. "Roman. Before that happens, my goal is to make you a part of his team. He doesn't deserve you, but you deserve to be treated as the princess you are."

"It won't matter. Once he's back..."

"When he is, you must not let him know that you know the truth unless he tells you."

My chin dropped at the thought of my husband's return.

The impostor squeezed my hand. "I can't live another man's life through the eternity of my own."

"What do I call you?" I asked.

"What do you call Roman?"

"To his face?" I asked with a genuine grin.

A smile curled his lips, bringing life to his dark eyes in a way I didn't recognize but immediately adored.

Taking a step back, I curtsied. "Your Highness."

"And I you?"

"The usual titles in public. Lucille in private."

The man nodded. "Lucille, shall we dine?"

He didn't offer me his arm, but he did wait for me to be beside him. As he opened the door, I whispered, "What about the queen?"

He shook his head. "That is at the king's discretion. Currently, no."

"Does the king know I know?"

He shook his head.

That meant that throughout dinner we would need to pretend. I looked up at him. "I don't want to ruin this for you."

"Good," he replied with a grin. "I'm trying to avoid prison."

"Then you should have gone back to America." Those were my words, but with all my heart, I was glad he hadn't.

"Yesterday?" I whispered as we were descending the staircase. "You were at dinner last night." I looked up at his handsome face. "I didn't know."

"You barely looked my direction."

"I must keep from staring tonight."

CHAPTER 17

Oliver

It took every ounce of willpower within me not to touch Lucille, to simply place my hand in the small of her back as I'd done at the birthday celebration. I'd watched long hours of videos and had been told by Lady Caroline that not only did the princess and I have a tense relationship, we also didn't do public displays of affection.

From what I'd surmised, the prince and princess didn't do many private displays of affection either. That could account for the lack of heirs.

When I'd entered Lucille's suite, I'd done so to convince myself that I could stay in character. If I could convince Lucille that I was Roman, I could convince anyone. And as the harsh words left my lips, I detested the man I'd become more than before.

It was the princess's spirit that called to me.

She didn't apologize or wilt like a helpless flower. That was what I'd been told to expect. Instead, standing there in a pale green dress, she stood her ground. I should have walked away.

It was her comment that tugged at my heart.

Of course, she wasn't a dog, a bitch to come on command. The idea that she would even have that thought was more than I could take. I should have continued to walk away. Now the damage was done.

Entering the dining room, I tried to forget that Lucille knew my secret, while remembering to act aloof. As the butler stepped forward and pulled back Lucille's chair, I took the seat to her side. Soon, the king would be seated to my other side at the head of the table.

"Mum," I said, standing with a bow as the queen entered.

"Your Majesty," Lucille said, standing with a curtsy before taking her seat again.

"Lucille," the queen said as she took the seat across from me. "I hear you're leaving us, going back to Monovia."

"Yes, ma'am. The unrest has quieted."

The queen turned to me. "Your father told me about your speech to the Parliament, Roman. He is pleased."

I nodded, refusing to turn to my side to see the reaction of the woman there. She knew it was an impostor who addressed Parliament. As the queen continued to speak, I assessed what I had done. By involving Lucille in the charade, she was an accomplice. If I failed, she could be punished as I would be, imprisoned in an actual prison.

"Roman."

Lucille tapped my leg below the table.

"Sorry, Mum. My mind is wandering."

"I was asking you why you were sending Lucille to Annabella. Surely, it is better to have her near."

Oh, it was better. It was also hell.

"The duchess has her duties in Monovia." I turned to Lucille. "Is returning a problem?"

Her eyes barely met mine. "No, Your Highness."

"Where is Papa?" I asked.

"He will be here soon," the queen replied as the butler filled her cup with tea.

Once the king was present, the dining room busied with women and men bringing us our meal.

Keeping Lucille to my side helped me stay focused on the king and queen. Listening to King Theodore question Lucille about her duties in Monovia, I recalled my first meeting with the ruler of Molave.

"Are you taking me to my sentencing?" I asked Lord Martin as we traversed the long hallways of the palace. It was the same day I'd given my vow.

"Stay in character, Your Highness."

My circulation thumped in my ears as it would

prior to a live performance. "I thought he knew."

"He does."

"This is a test," I assessed as we entered the outer chamber to the king's study.

"Perhaps think of it as an audition."

Before I could respond to Lord Martin, the woman behind a desk stood and curtsied, calling me your highness.

"A very important one, sir," Lord Martin replied softly.

I took a deep breath and turned to the woman. "The king requested my presence."

"He is waiting for you, Your Highness."

"Then get on with it." I stepped toward the double doors. When I turned back, Lord Martin nodded.

The woman opened the door and curtsied to the king. "Your Grace, Prince Roman is here."

"Yes, yes," the king replied, waving me in.

I tried not to marvel at my proximity to Theodore Godfrey III. I'd been studying him as well as his son for nearly over a month, and while I stood by my assessment that Molave was a strange world within itself, I also recognized the power the man before me held. He'd sat at tables with rulers, presidents, and prime ministers from all over the globe. He'd brought his country into the modern world while maintaining its sovereignty. He was beloved and revered.

Stepping forward, the woman closed the door behind me, leaving me alone with King Theodore. I bowed at the waist. "Papa."

His dark eyes narrowed as they swept over me. Finally, he spoke. "Come, have a seat, boy."

Boy.

Roman Godfrey was a forty-three-year-old man, the first in line for the seat across the desk.

King Theodore leaned back in his chair. "Tell me what you know."

"I know a wide range of things."

He lifted a paper from his blotter and turned it my direction. It was the paper the chief minister had me sign.

"Your Majesty," I said.

Placing the paper on the desk, he leaned forward. "No one will see that from this day forward if things continue as planned."

I nodded.

"I know why Elizabeth thought you would be best for this role. However, these are very unusual times. I'm not pleased that my son isn't the man to step up." His gaze honed in on mine. "Tell me why you are that man. Why are you willing to sacrifice your life for Molave?"

Stay in character.

I sat taller. "It is my duty."

"You are not Molavian."

"As your son..."

The king grinned. "My son would not have replied as politely."

"I'm still learning, sir."

"You're aware of what's happening in the streets?"

"I'm aware of the unrest due to the recently sanctioned tariffs. I've just moments ago received clearance to learn the reason behind the tariffs as well as other vital information."

"You will come to me each evening at five thirty, here in my office. We have a standing meeting. Thirty minutes. It is all we'll need. You will talk to me about what you've learned, and I will inform you of new developments."

"The prince...?"

"At five thirty he is retired to his apartments, preparing for our evening dinner. You will be free to walk through the palace without question."

I nodded.

The king's gaze again narrowed. "You have passed the point of no return."

"I'm aware. Your health?" I asked.

"Is my son asking?"

"Shouldn't he care?"

"He should. The reports are exaggerated. I am stronger each day."

"That is good to hear, sir."

"*Anne didn't mention her conversation with you at the young prince's birthday. That means she thought nothing of it. After seeing you, I can understand why.*"

"*It is an honor—*"

"*No, son, it is a duty. Do not look upon me, your mother, or any other world leader or dignitary with honor. Each one thinks they're more important, more unique, more special than they are. Everyone can be replaced. After all, we're all replacements of another. Success comes in the right replacement. Your role... Roman's role*" —he emphasized— "*is to understand that. I hope that he will, sooner rather than later.*"

"*Once he does...?*"

"*You will be dismissed with a substantial payment and a vow of secrecy.*"

Hearing those words was a relief to say the least.

The king's answer meant that there was an end to this road, one that hopefully didn't stop at a Molavian prison.

"*Tomorrow, five thirty.*"

"*Yes, sir.*"

"*And when I ask what you know, I expect a well-thought-out answer.*"

I nodded.

"*Tell Lord Martin he passed.*"

"*He?*" I grinned.

"*I wish I could tell you that what you're doing will*

end at a particular date. I cannot. Much depends on Roman, the damage he's done and his willingness to repent. In the meantime, the world must see him as an active participant in Molavian as well as European and world affairs. Molave needs him to be seen."

"Yes, sir, I will be seen."

"Your accent is uncanny. If I didn't know..." He grinned before asking me one last question—was I confident in this position? He didn't speak the question in English but in Norwegian.

I responded in the same language, assuring him that I was and would continue to learn all that I could.

That meeting was two weeks ago yesterday. Each evening at five thirty, I presented myself to his office and briefed the king on my acquired knowledge. Either he would discuss the matters I mentioned or discuss more recent happenings.

Two days ago, I was informed I would be moved to the prince's suite.

The curtain had not only risen on this performance but had been ripped from its valance, leaving it in a perpetually opened state.

Lucille stood, placing her napkin on the bottom edge of her plate. After a curtsy, she nodded to the king and queen. "If you'll excuse me, I have a trip to take."

"What is the harm in one more night?" Queen Anne asked.

"I should—"

"You may leave in the morning," I said, interrupting the princess. My voice stayed steady, calm, and dry, yet my heart was beating at untold speed. If it were not for the padded shirt, it would probably be visible.

Queen Anne smiled. "There. That wasn't difficult." Her focus went to Lucille's plate. "Oh dear, you didn't eat. I was so happy with your recently improved appetite."

"Too many cakes at tea, Your Majesty." Lucille curtsied again. "I look forward to seeing you both soon, if it is to be."

I watched as Lucille departed without a word to me. With her posture straight and chin held high, she was the epitome of everything I imagined a princess to be—without the joyfulness Disney liked to include.

Once Lucille was gone, the queen looked my way. "You should take her some cake. Eating is essential to a healthy pregnancy."

Pushing my chair back, I threw my napkin on my plate as I stood. "Really, Mum. Stop."

Her lips pursed and her neck straightened. "Roman, you're sending her away."

My volume rose. "It is my concern, not yours."

"Roman," the king admonished.

It was almost comical the tolerance that everyone

bestowed on the prince's outbursts. Maybe I'd talk to the chief minister about an appointment with the royal physician. There were medications that could bring Roman down a notch or two.

"I'm going out to the gardens."

With that, I turned and walked away from the king and queen. As I was walking through the multiple parlors on my way to a door leading to the gardens, Lord Martin appeared.

"Your Highness. Is all well?"

"I need air."

With a bow, he allowed me passage.

While the temperature was lower than it had been during the day, the absence of rain made my stroll comfortable. My options were limited. I could go to Roman's offices, to the one where the classified documents were now held. However, that would require contacting the chief minister for a deputy. I'd also been told that wasn't the prince's normal routine.

I couldn't go up to the apartments, knowing Lucille was close. It was difficult enough last night when she didn't know that I wasn't Roman.

It didn't help that the queen had basically commanded that I bed my wife.

My walking stopped as I turned toward the gazebo. "Princess."

Her blue stare came my way. "Your Highness."

CHAPTER
18

Lucille

With my hands gripping the railing, I waited as Roman came closer. I scanned from his hair to his shoes, looking for anything that would alert anyone to his deception. The resemblance was uncanny. As he neared, I longed to ask his real name. However, common sense told me that if I thought of him as Roman and spoke to him as Roman, no one would be the wiser.

"Do you come out here often?" he asked, stepping into the gazebo.

"I used to. Before we were married." I turned and smiled. "You know what I mean."

"I wasn't looking for you."

My smile dimmed. "You weren't?"

He shook his head. "Not because I don't want to see you. I wasn't looking for you because I want to see you more than I should. Monovia is the best place for you while I perfect this role." He looked out into the gardens and back to me. "I read where you lived here in the palace before your wedding."

"I did. Not in the royal wing. During that time, I had visions of princes and princesses. Every American thinks they understand royalty, but they don't, not really. No one can tell you what it's like."

"You can tell me," he said, reaching for my hand and tugging me toward the cement bench.

Smoothing my skirt from behind, I sat. The sight of my shoes made me grin. "I wore shoes this time."

"I was afraid you'd become ill. It was downright frigid that night."

"Your coat helped."

Roman turned my direction. "I believe I've made a dreadful mistake."

I sucked in a breath. "Oh no. Does the queen suspect?"

"No. My mistake was being honest with you. In doing so, I've put you in possible danger. If this ends poorly..."

I tilted my head. "Don't let it end poorly."

"I appreciate your confidence."

"You give me more than that, Roman." I took a breath. "May we agree to use his name? I'd hate to slip if I knew yours."

He nodded. "What do I give you, Lucille?"

"Hope. Hope for Molave. Hope for me. It's something I'd let slip away." I sat taller. "I came out here to avoid you, not wanting to face you in the apartments."

His smile grew. "I had the same reasoning."

My gaze went to his. "I want to help you. I don't know how."

"Talk to me. Tell me what I can't learn in classified documents or from watching videos. I've received so much advice that sometimes I feel like I'm him." He scoffed. "And if Roman doesn't start taking some anti-anxiety medications soon, I'll need to."

My giggle bubbled out of me.

It had been too long since I'd felt free enough to giggle in the prince's presence. "I think everyone would be pleased with that decision, Your Highness."

"Don't you get lonely?"

I turned to him, seeing the concern in his dark stare. "Horribly."

"Has it really been a year since you've seen your parents?"

I nodded. "I speak to them weekly—mostly my mother."

"Do they know how sad you've been?"

Standing, I walked to the railing. While this Roman's ability to see me was new and intriguing, it was also upsetting. How could this man who barely knew me see me when my husband didn't?

"Sir, you don't know me." I spun toward him. "I was raised with a sense of duty, not to Molave, but to use my advantages to help others. My mother is a shining example." A memory came to mind. "Do you know where we would spend Thanksgivings when I was a child?"

With his concentration solely on me, Roman shook his head.

"There was a particular homeless mission in the city."

"New York?"

"Yes. We went every year. When I was young, I complained that we didn't celebrate the holiday the way my friends did with family and feasts." I smiled. "And then it became a tradition I savored. The people we served never knew our names. It was fun each time to come up with a new pseudonym. My mom made it a game."

"Why didn't you use your real names?"

"My dad said that people would look at us as if we were campaigning for him." It occurred to me that he might not know what my father did. "He's a United States senator."

Roman nodded. "And your mother is a baroness from Borinkia."

"It wasn't Borinkia then, when her family fled to the US. It was still Letanonia."

Standing, the man came closer. "Please tell me more."

"My father, he didn't want what we did out of a sense of duty to be misconstrued. The year before you and I wed was the last time I worked in that kitchen." A bubble of happiness grew within me at the memories. "That year, over ten thousand meals were served. My mother's foundation supplied the food and paper products. She also supported that shelter throughout the year."

"Your mother's foundation. Surely, they knew who you were."

"The people running the shelter, yes. They never shared our secret." My smile dimmed as I sighed. "I guess I thought as a sovereign, I would have the opportunity to help or even to make a difference."

"I'm sorry, Lucille."

I looked up at the man now at my side. "Don't say that. Roman would never say that. He never has. You said it tonight to the queen. He wouldn't even do that."

"Then I will only utter it when we're in private."

"We rarely are. Lady Buckingham would instantly pick up on a slip like that."

"She sees everything?" he asked, reaching for my chin and lifting my face toward his.

"Yes."

"As long as I'm here, she will never see another bruise."

I scoffed. "That might cause questions too."

"I'm serious, Lucille. I admire your commitment to Molave, to the crown, and even to Roman. I will make you a promise."

"Don't. If you make a promise, you could break it. For the last few weeks, you have been my" —I searched for the right words— "my secret and my sustenance. You filled a void that was consuming me. I savored every moment of our frigid nighttime conversation. If you make me a promise and break it, then I will have nothing."

His finger came gently to my lips. "I want a promise in return." Without allowing me to speak, he went on in Roman's voice, with Roman's appearance, and surrounded by the familiar scent of his cologne. However, the words were not what Roman would say. "I will do my best to treat you the way you should be treated. I will keep my vow to Molave and the king. Once Roman returns, your promise to me is that you seriously reevaluate your vows."

I took a deep breath.

"Lucille, if he doesn't value you as you should be, you promise me that you will consider returning to America." He lowered his finger.

"With you?" I scoffed. "Wouldn't we be the talk of the town?"

"Not with me. Remember what it was like being the young girl in a large New York City shelter. That girl had to be strong and determined to not be frightened."

"It wasn't frightening. It wasn't even" —I thought about it— "it wasn't a burden or a penitence for being affluent. It was a gift to see the world that so many people choose to ignore."

"You are beautiful. Your heart is even more beautiful."

Warmth filled my cheeks.

"Remember that young girl, Lucille. If you aren't helping people here, you could back in the States."

A new thought came to me. "I've never told Roman that story."

"Why?"

"He doesn't listen." I spun toward the railing, afraid to keep looking into his gaze. "Roman doesn't listen to anyone. Tonight, with King Theo, you were more attentive than Roman would be."

"I'm doing my best to be an asshole."

A smile curled my lips. "You'll need to work harder." I stepped back and walked all the way around Roman, looking at him from all directions. "Did they change your appearance or are you a doppelgänger?"

He smiled. "I'm younger. My hair is usually shorter, and I don't have natural gray."

I waved my hand up and down. "The Firm has done an amazing job."

Small lines of concern appeared near his eyes. "I never mentioned…"

"You didn't need to. Once Queen Anne mentioned that you spoke to Parliament, I knew you had to have the Firm's approval. There's no other possibility. I just don't understand what Roman's done to lose their approval."

"If the day comes that I learn that information and I am able to tell you, I will."

Bowing my head, I looked up with a smile. "Thank you, Your Highness. That's more of a promise than I've ever had before."

The weight of his stare caused my breath to stagger. The intensity was overwhelming as if I were my husband's lifeline. No, he wasn't my husband.

It was my last thought before he wrapped his arm around my waist and his lips collided with mine. Unlike the last time we were in the gazebo, this kiss was passionate, strong, and enticing. As our heads turned one way and the next and our lips sought one another's, I forgot that this was wrong.

My hands reached up to his shoulders, my fingers through his hair. He pulled me closer, my breasts flattening upon his chest. I felt the tempo of his pulse through the tips of my fingers as the heat between us caused sparks to ignite into flames, sweeping through me like a forest fire in dry underbrush.

When we came up for air, I took a step back and away, my chin falling to my chest.

Roman reached for my chin, bringing my gaze to his. "That is why you should leave."

"You're right."

A smile blossomed on his lips. "The queen basically instructed me to go upstairs and bed you."

"Did the king intervene?"

"No, I rebuked her and stormed away."

His response made me smile. "That was very Roman."

"Will I see you before you leave in the morning?"

I shook my head. "It wouldn't be natural."

"I'd like to walk with you back to the apartments."

Again, I shook my head. "You are what I wish Roman could be, but you're not him. I'm married."

He took a step back. "You're right, Princess."

"I wish I wasn't." I took a deep breath. "He does occasionally call me while he's away."

"Are the lines secure?"

"I think." I shrugged. "I don't know. It would still be nice to receive a call, to know you are safe and things are well. We can maintain the façade in case anyone is listening."

"Don't worry about me."

"I already am," I said, taking another step back. With a quick curtsy, I smiled. "Good night, my prince."

He bowed. "My princess."

CHAPTER
19

"You will return to Molave City," Roman declared as soon as our call connected. At only nine in the morning, it wasn't what I expected.

It had been two weeks since I'd made the two-hour trip to Monovia, to Annabella Castle. While my husband and I spoke with some regularity, with my technology still shielded and the concern that our calls were overheard, I was at a loss for what was happening in Molave with Roman or the government issues at hand. Despite the previous unrest being resolved, the king requested that I stay safe within the castle walls.

As with all royal requests, it was a mandate.

For fourteen days, I'd wandered the hallways and tended to what remained of my gardens upon the grounds. The sweltering summer heat while on our Eurasia tour was long gone. While the calendar only warned of autumn, soon the snow would begin to fly, especially in the higher elevations.

"Your Highness?" I responded.

"Today."

"Is there a problem?"

His curt response caught me off guard. "Only that you're questioning me. I've instructed the guards at Annabella. No traveling in unsafe cars. You will travel in the royal fleet."

I looked down at my dressing gown. With no one but Lady Buckingham and the rest of the castle staff in my presence, I lacked the motivation to rise and dress. "I will alert my mistress."

"Send a text message when you leave Annabella."

The fear of nonsecure phone service made me choose my words carefully. "Roman, will I see you?"

"Yes, we need to speak—in person."

The little bit of breakfast I'd consumed churned in my stomach as the phone in my hand went dead. There was much I could infer from Roman's tone if it were truly Roman. The impostor was usually steadier and less abrasive. That meant that either the real Roman was back or that my impostor was concerned.

Both options filled me with equal portions of dread.

Pushing the button on the table in my library, I waited until the door opened.

"Your Highness," Geoffrey said, clasping his hands behind his back after the bow of his head.

"Tell Lady Buckingham I request her presence."

Geoffrey nodded.

"And Geoffrey, alert the guards my mistress and I will be traveling to Molave City as soon as we can collect our things."

"The prince already called, Your Highness. They are getting the fleet together."

Roman called the guards before he called me?

"Good," I said with a nod.

Minutes later, there was a knock as Lady Buckingham entered the library.

"We're going back to Molave City," I said after her usual salute.

"I was told." Her expression showed the concern her words didn't say.

"I don't know," I replied, answering her unspoken question. "Roman just called and told me to come. Do you know more than I? Are there troubles again?"

"Not that I'm aware of." She shrugged. "Nothing out of the ordinary."

"I will dress, and we will go."

"Do you have any idea how long your presence will be required?"

"I don't know anything other than Roman sounded...he sounded concerned. He insisted that we travel in the royal fleet."

"Concerned," she mumbled before meeting my gaze.

"Lady Buckingham," I addressed her in a rare

rebuke. "Roman Godfrey is the prince. For that reason alone, he will receive our respect."

Bowing her head, she curtsied. "I apologize, Your Highness. If you'll accompany me to your suite, I'll assist you in dressing for the day. I'll also instruct the maids to pack your things."

As Lady Buckingham tended to my makeup and dressing, my thoughts were consumed with the strange concoction of equal parts anticipation and apprehension.

"There is something," she began to say, speaking softly.

There was a quality to her tone that made the small hairs on the back of my neck stand to attention. "Go on."

"I was just made aware of a search conducted here at Annabella."

My eyes opened wide. "When?"

"While we were in Molave City."

"By whom?"

"Deputies of the Ministry."

My eyebrows knitted together. "Here?" The new Roman came to mind.

Did someone suspect I knew?

No, I didn't know of him when I traveled to the palace for Rothy's birthday. I didn't know, but by his own account he was there in Molave City.

I tried to recall returning to Annabella Castle. "Nothing was out of the ordinary."

"No, Your Highness. I'm telling you because perhaps you're being called away so another search may be conducted."

Standing, I let my focus roam around my private parlor. "There is nothing here."

Lady Buckingham nodded. "I wasn't told what they were seeking or even where they searched."

An hour later, sitting with my mistress in the back seat of one of the reinforced royal vehicles, I had a new thought. Keeping my volume low, I asked, "Could it be routine, and we were never made aware in the past?"

"The search?"

I nodded.

"Perhaps," she replied. "Please, Princess, don't worry about it. The king, the chief minister, and their representatives have the discretion to enter royal property. You, Your Highness, have nothing to hide."

Her words of encouragement rang false with my knowledge of the new Roman. Of course, I'd hidden that knowledge where no search would find it, in my thoughts and possibly my heart. I'd never be careless enough to commit my feelings to pen and paper. As a young girl, I'd wanted a diary. My mother's stories of fleeing Letanonia as the new ruler searched for evidence of crimes or anything to be used against the wealthy families convinced me to never write down my daily thoughts. "Hold them in your heart," she told me. "No one can use them against you there."

Lady Buckingham covered my hand with one of hers, bringing my attention to the present.

"You're strong, Princess. I've seen the change in you since we returned to Annabella. If it truly is the prince who wants something of you, you will provide."

"I think it's not knowing what he wants that concerns me."

There were no large crowds as we left the castle grounds or protests blocking traffic. When we entered Molave City, our cars were met by multiple vehicles, no doubt filled with royal guards, and escorted onto the palace grounds.

My pulse raced and my skin grew clammy as I nodded to the palace staff. In the grand entry, I looked up toward the staircase, sensing the stare of the man above. With no more than a flick of his chin, Roman bid me upstairs. My eyes met Lady Buckingham's.

"I will—"

I shook my head. "No, leave us. He called and he's waiting. It's my duty to find out what he wants."

With each stair my apprehension grew as anticipation waned.

There was no way to prepare for what I didn't know.

Who will the man be in our private quarters?

Is the real Roman back?

Does he know of the plan and wants to know if I know?

My grip trembled upon the large knob as I turned it and pushed the tall door inward. Standing near the fireplace, Roman turned my direction, his stare dark and focused.

Curtsying, I spoke, "Your Highness."

He came my way. "Lady Buckingham?"

"I told her to allow us privacy."

Coming across the room, Roman closed the door behind me with a slam, reached for me, and wrapped me in an embrace as his lips took mine. The ferocity of his approach had me again questioning his identity. It wasn't until he spoke that I knew whose arms I was in. "There is so much I need to tell you."

My entire body melted, the tension of the unknown washing away in my exhale. Palming his cheeks, I looked up at his handsome face and smiled. "It's as if you're really him, and you have two personalities. I truly can't tell."

His finger landed on my lips and his volume lowered to a whisper. "We have to be careful."

I nodded.

Roman reached for my hand and tugged me toward his suite.

At the double doors, I stopped. "I cannot."

"You are my wife," he said in a bellowing tone. As he led me within, he added, "We will only talk. I believe the entire apartment is safe. I've done my best to check for cameras or microphones. I know the private quarters are secure. I've had it confirmed."

Never in five years had that occurred to me.

"Who would be watching?" I asked.

"The Firm. The king. There are many possibilities."

Releasing my hand, Roman paced to the fireplace in his parlor and back. When his stare met mine, I saw the concern. It was more than his appearance. While this man had said he was younger than Roman, in the short period I'd been gone, he aged. There was a tenseness to his jaw and a weariness in his eyes.

"What is it?"

Such a simple question and yet not one I would dare present to the real prince.

"If I could, I'd put us both on a plane to America and never come back."

"I don't understand."

"I don't either, not completely," he said, leading me to the sofa. "I told the king I was calling you here because we have a visitor arriving early tomorrow and you can be of assistance."

"A visitor?"

"Your father."

I sucked in a breath. "My father is coming here. Why? Is my mother coming?"

"No. And according to palace records, he was here last spring."

I shook my head. "No. I would have been told."

"Lucille, I need your help. I'm good. I'm damn good, but I can't discuss what I don't know."

The disbelief of his announcement had me scrambled. "You and my father get along. You think he's too lenient with my mother. He thinks you're pompous."

"Has he said as much?"

"Not to me. I see it in the way he looks at you."

Roman's forehead furrowed. "What do you know of their business dealings?"

"Nothing. There are none." I stood and walked to the window and back. "Roman's never mentioned one if it exists."

"There is. It began as an arrangement for your hand."

"No," I said dismissively. "I was informed that my father and King Theo arranged for Roman and I to meet. I wasn't forced to marry him. At the time, I wanted to."

"Lucille, there's much more to this that I am only now learning. Your father established a beneficial connection when you agreed to marry Roman. Molave and the US signed an agreement for the export of iron ore and titanium. You probably know, but those as well as other metals, when combined in high-performance alloys, are used in cell phones, jet engines, military equipment such as weapons, and body armor. It was a large win for the US military as well as for Molave. There was more, an agreement for osmium, iridium, and rhodium. The scarcity of rhodium makes it valuable."

"I don't know anything about this agreement."

"The king was able to give me the information on the original deal. Molave got you" —his nostrils flared— "Roman got you. King Theodore agreed to a seven-year deal at over fifteen billion dollars from the US. Your father earned a large dividend for his campaign. The senator added the measure to an already-vetted bill. It passed without further debate. It consisted of two sentences that weren't noticed until the bill was law. Despite that, it has had little blowback."

"Seven years?"

"Yes, seven years. Set to expire in less than a year. Roman was in negotiations with your father regarding continuing the deal. There are no records of those negotiations. There are phone records that give dates and the length of the call, but nothing of substance noted. No tapes to hear. Senator Sutton is coming tomorrow because he wants to resolve this face-to-face before the appropriations committee steps in. From what I understand, he wants it to continue under the radar."

"My father is not a bad man," I said.

"Lucille, he used you as a pawn to get resources to the US, earn a huge stipend, and simultaneously pad the Molavian royal treasury."

"Surely, King Theo—"

"No," Roman interrupted. "He's concerned. Your father isn't the only person Roman dealt with, unbeknownst to the king. This particular contract is substantial and with recent titanium discoveries in Greenland..." He sighed. "The king doesn't want to lose it, but neither of us nor any of the advisors know what was discussed."

"The king could learn the truth from Roman."

The man at my side stood and exhaled.

"What is it?" I asked, standing and reaching for his arm. "Is Roman safe?"

He reached for my shoulders and lifted his eyebrows. "I'm being honest with you, Lucille. I don't know. I suggested the same thing, and the king said it was my responsibility."

"Your responsibility," I repeated. "To fix what Roman broke? He's testing you."

Roman nodded.

"How do you want me to help?" I asked.

"Calm the waters with your father."

"Roman, he won't tell me anything about the deal. He never discussed senate affairs with me, even when I was attending Columbia. If I had a particular question, he would answer. This is different."

My husband's smile returned. "I have a plan."

CHAPTER 20

Oliver

"The king knows you're involving me?" Lucille asked, her blue eyes wide.

"The king doesn't know that you're aware of the plan the Firm has in place."

"The plan being you." She didn't ask as much as confirm.

I nodded. "However, as I promised you, I want to help you take on more as princess." My cheeks rose as I smiled. "You are much more than an accessory. Here is a chance to prove it."

"And he agreed?"

"He agreed to allow you to return and to see your father. I told him of your disappointment with the trip to the US being held off. He agreed. The particulars were not discussed."

Lucille took a deep breath, the color draining from her cheeks as she sat back down on the sofa, crossed her ankles. When her gaze met mine, she nodded. "Tell me your plan."

For the next thirty minutes, I explained what I knew and how I thought it would work for her to take part. In a nutshell, I'd give Senator Sutton some bullshit story about the princess wanting to be involved in state affairs and how I didn't agree; however, I acquiesced in this instance because he as her father wouldn't tell the world if she failed.

"You think I'll fail?"

"No, Princess, I think you're more than capable. Your father is a safe audience. Utilize whatever technique you must. Blame me. Tell him how important it is to you to be involved. Speak of this after I'm called away. If my plan works, you will have the details before I return. Give me clues. I can improvise enough to take us to intermission."

Lucille's smile took my breath away. "Acting."

"Acting. The only problem with this gig is if we don't succeed, we'll face more than a lousy review."

She reached for my hand. "Then we will succeed."

I looked down at our union, feeling the warmth from her soft skin and back up to her sensational smile. "I think this is the first time you reached out to me."

"You reached out to me, Roman. You called and I came. If I can help keep you safe, in King Theo's good graces, and help Molave at the same time, I will. Helping you is all I've ever wanted to do."

Taking a deep breath, I leaned forward, kissing her

cheek. "We've already spent too much time alone. Lady Buckingham will be suspicious."

"I have a plan."

My curiosity grew as Lucille led me back to the bedchamber. Her smile glistened as she reached for the buttons on my suit coat. "You said you take clues. If you leave clues, it won't be suspicious."

Tugging the jacket from my shoulders, she let it drop to the floor and reached for my tie.

"Fuck, Lucille."

"Shh. You forgot your accent."

"We can't...You said..." So much for being an extraordinary orator. As the princess slid the tie from around my neck, my accent was back, yet I was nothing more than a stuttering fraud.

Next, she pulled back the bedclothes and messed the pillows. It was after she'd removed her boots and reached for the buttons on her sweater that she looked up. With pink-filled cheeks, she said, "Turn around."

My heart raced and my mouth dried as I imagined that she was about to undress. "Not that I'm not one hundred percent in favor of you stripping before me, but surely, Lady Buckingham won't believe..."

"That you called me here for sex?" Her smile grew. "That she will believe. That you called me here to help you with matters of state, she'll tell you that I've officially gone mad and have me committed before dinner."

Lucille twirled her finger, gesturing for me to turn.

Pivoting, I faced the wall.

It didn't matter how many Molavian facts I tried to recite, with each passing moment as a sweater, slacks, socks...dear Lord above, a bra, and lastly, white lace panties littered the carpet, my body was inappropriately coming to life.

"You may turn."

I sucked in a breath as Lucille leaned against the headboard, her body covered with blankets to above her breasts. Her long hair was loose and mussed.

"You're fucking beautiful."

"Thank you, Your Highness." Her head tilted. "Perhaps you could untuck your shirt. And when you exit the room, be upset."

"Why the hell would I be upset?"

"We had an argument."

Pulling the shirt tails from my trousers, I met her gaze. "You don't exactly look like we had an argument."

"Yes," she said, looking down at her arms and shoulders. "I could use a bit of help."

"I mean, if you want to make this real..."

She shook her head. "Not real. Believable. If you'd kiss me as you did when I arrived. And my neck and shoulders...your whiskers. My skin reddens easily."

"If the king..." I said.

"He won't. If there is anything that you need to know about this life, it's that I'm invisible."

"No, Lucille. I'm standing here looking at you, and you are about as far from invisible as possible. Honestly, if we're being real. I want to help you, but damn, I'm hard and..." I stepped closer.

She patted the bed beside her. "Acting."

"Acting," I repeated, sitting at her side.

Hell, I'd never had an erection like this while filming sex scenes. Of course, there had been twenty-five people, cameras, and hot lights. This was a bit different.

I leaned forward, my lips meeting hers. Lucille met me with equal force as I tugged on her long hair. Pushing me away, Lucille directed my attention lower. As she held my head, I delivered kisses and nips to her neck and shoulders.

"Rougher."

I looked up, meeting her gaze. "I hate him."

"This isn't about him. It's about you and acting."

"Acting," I repeated again.

As Princess Lucille writhed in my grasp, I continued my ministrations. Beneath my touch her soft, sensitive flesh reddened in splotches. By some grace of God, I didn't come in my slacks. That didn't mean I wasn't painfully hard. As I stood, I couldn't help but adjust myself.

Lucille laughed.

"You think this is funny?"

"No. Yes. Come here."

She reached up and unbuttoned the top two buttons of my shirt.

"What is this?" Her fingers were touching the padding beneath.

"My...well, my body's shape is different than his."

Bowing her head, she veiled her beautiful eyes. "From what I can tell, in more ways than one." She looked up. "Take your jacket and tie and don't forget to be angry."

"You?"

"Sad."

"I hate this," I admitted.

"I don't. You asked for my help. This is part of it. Be short with whoever is present in the parlor. Loud even. Send Lady Buckingham to me."

I reached for her hand. "Tonight, after dinner, the gazebo."

"Yes, Your Highness."

My kisses to her knuckles were gentle.

Picking up my suit coat and tie, I spent too long staring down at the pile of Lucille's clothes. When I looked back at her, the last emotion I had was anger.

"Go," she said, "I'm having trouble being sad with you here."

"What did we argue about?"

"We argue about everything...when we actually speak. Usually, there isn't a lot of talking." She looked down at her shoulder. "Hurry, or we'll have to start over."

"As if that is supposed to make me want to leave."

"I'm always asking you to allow me to help. You won't entertain the thought of it."

Closing my eyes, I sighed. Raising my volume I said, "No more talk. Your duty..."

Lucille nodded, her expression souring as she scooted down beneath the covers and turned her face into a pillow.

I continued a tirade as I slammed the door to the bedchamber. It was as I opened the one to the connecting parlor that I came eye to eye with Lady Buckingham. With a grunt, I tucked my shirt into my trousers and pushed my arms into the suit-coat sleeves.

"Your Highness." She curtsied. "Lord Martin said to tell you that he will be in your offices."

Huffing, I tilted my head toward the suite. "The princess is in need of your assistance."

"Yes, Your Highness."

Stepping to the mirror over the fireplace, I adjusted my tie and jacket, reminding my reflection that I was angry. It was a good thing that I was an actor by profession because as my erection softened to a manageable appendage, I was reaching for the years of training. Instead of grunting like a boorish rake, I wanted to smile from ear to ear.

Thoughts of Senator Sutton's arrival and our plan made me sober as I made my way to Roman's offices.

CHAPTER 21

Lucille

With a cagoule wrapped around me, I made my way through the mist to the gazebo, barely noticing the alterations to the gardens that came with the change of season. After dinner, I'd gone to my suite and changed from my dress back into the clothes I'd worn to travel. When Lady Buckingham questioned my destination, I simply stated that I wanted to walk in the gardens. After having found me upset this afternoon, no other explanation was needed.

Despite the chill, I found myself elated for my upcoming clandestine meeting. It took all my focus at dinner to remain aloof. Since my last meal at the palace, Roman had made progress in perfecting his inattentiveness. If it were not so serious, I would be able to laugh.

Rounding the bend, my anticipation morphed to disappointment at the sight of the empty gazebo. I wondered if perhaps I'd taken too long in changing clothes, if Roman was called away, or if he was delayed. Hoping for the latter, I sat on the concrete bench and concentrated on the freedom granted within the palace gardens while at the same time refusing to admit that I wanted to see the new Roman.

As I'd told him the night of his confession, it was almost as if he were conjured in my mind, a husband who not only saw me but also listened. And when I believed he was gone, I'd held tight to the memory. A smile curled my lips as I looked down at my boots. I wouldn't be chilled as I was that first night.

Thoughts went to the way he wrapped me in his jacket, the warmth from his body and scent of his cologne.

From there, my thoughts wandered to this afternoon. Closing my eyes, I remembered the sensation of his kisses. His touch was the opposite of the man he resembled—almost reverent. With nothing more than acting, I was immediately addicted. While I'd told myself we were pretending, I heard my own sounds, noises I couldn't control as well as the rush of heat as my insides twisted, and moisture dampened my core.

"Lucille."

The deep, booming voice of the king pulled me from my trance.

"Your Majesty," I said, standing and curtsying. My

cheeks warmed as if I'd been caught, a schoolgirl fantasizing about what she shouldn't.

"What are you doing out in this cold?"

"I enjoy the palace gardens," I said truthfully. "I began coming out here before my marriage. It's peaceful."

The king stepped up the stairs as I took him in. His once-dark hair, now more white than black, was covered by a cap. His cheeks were pink from the cold, giving him a healthier appearance. The thick jumper he wore over his shirt sparkled with droplets of rain.

"Quite right," King Theo said. "I've always enjoyed an evening stroll, even when the weather isn't favorable."

I nodded my head, wondering if there was an unspoken meaning.

Had the king seen Roman and me out here?

King Theo motioned to the concrete bench. "Since we're here, I'd like to speak."

My stomach twisted as I agreed and sat.

His voice was customarily pleasant with a smidgen of seriousness. "What we are about to discuss is a matter of classified information."

"Sir, perhaps this should be discussed with the prince."

"The topic of this discussion is the prince."

Holding my own hands so as to stop them from

visibly trembling, I nodded. "Your Grace, I will hold whatever information you want to discuss in my heart for eternity."

His jovial laugh filled the air as his breath created a cloud of condensation. "It's not that serious, my dear. And yet it is. How has Roman seemed to you?"

I looked down at my lap. "The same. We rarely speak."

"And why is that?"

Looking back up, I met his dark stare. "I'm uncomfortable discussing our personal interaction, sir."

"Has he confided anything to you?"

I shook my head. "I'm at a loss, sir. Are you asking of ever or of recently?"

The king inhaled, pushing up from his thighs and sitting taller. "Ever. About his future as the king."

"Only that he is proud to do his duty. He did say..." I stopped.

"Go on."

"When the tariffs were in place" —I shrugged— "perhaps they still are. I wasn't informed. During the unrest, Roman mentioned that he didn't want Molave to lose financial standing on his watch."

"Have you known him to write, say, journals or the like? Some rulers see themselves as too important to not record daily happenings."

I shook my head as I thought back. "Not that I've seen. Even at Annabella, the prince enjoys time alone."

"His offices?"

"Or his suite."

"And when he's not there, do you frequent those areas?"

I shook my head again. "No. I realize they aren't locked, but I don't enter without the prince's invitation."

The king stood and turned. "Lucille, this next subject is also personal, but it is a matter of state. The royal physicians have discussed with Roman and he with me that you may have a better chance of conceiving with what the physicians refer to as IUI."

My breath caught. I had a flash of a memory of Roman mentioning that, but I'd forgotten with all that was currently occurring.

"Of course," the king went on, "no one would know how the heir was conceived."

Standing, I lifted my chin. "I do believe this is a discussion for the prince and me."

"You said you don't speak. I wasn't certain if he'd told you that you have an appointment to see Mr. Davies."

The head royal physician.

Over the last five years, I'd been seen by Mr. Davies as well as other specialists, all searching for the answer of why I hadn't conceived. The idea of another examination caused the dinner I'd eaten earlier to churn.

"An appointment? When?"

"Tomorrow."

"My father?" I tried, searching for a reason to postpone.

"Senator Sutton will be here in the afternoon, after your appointment."

"Afternoon? Roman mentioned he would arrive in the morning." I honestly wasn't considering my words. The idea of conceiving a child in a scientific manner had me troubled. "That was why Roman called me here, to see my father. It has been over a year."

The king's smile returned. "It seems you two do speak."

Shit.

I'd said too much.

Taking a breath and curtsying, I added with a grin, "Your Grace, I believe Roman was pacifying me. I truly have pestered him to allow me to take a trip to America."

"It would be better to wait until after the holidays. There are too many issues at hand."

"Yes, that's what Roman said."

"Lady Kornhall will inform Lady Buckingham of the details regarding your appointment."

"Of course, sir."

The king looked around the sides of the gazebo. "It's far too cool for me to leave you outside." He offered me his arm. "Let us get to the warmth of the palace."

Laying my hand on his arm, I nodded. The king spoke of flowering bushes and changing weather as we traversed the garden paths. With my gaze mostly down, I wondered if Roman was near, if he'd heard our conversation. Discussing my inability to conceive was a delicate subject with the real prince, and one I found too personal for a man I'd just met.

"...consider staying in Molave City. The weather prognosticators are predicting an unusually heavy snowfall in the elevations. Monovia could be covered in a meter of snow."

"If it is your wish, Your Grace."

"My concern is for your safety, Lucille. You are not a prisoner in the palace. If going back to Monovia is your wish, please do so before the first snow." He grinned. "Historically, the early snowfalls don't last too long. The temperature will rise, and travel will again be safe."

"Good night, Your Grace," I said with a bow of my head as we entered the palace and warm air caused the king's glasses to fog.

"I would not be offended, Lucille, to hear you call me Papa in private."

It was never a title I'd assumed. I referred to my father as Dad, a different endearment for the man who had always been supportive and loving was welcomed.

"It would be an honor." My smile grew. "Good night, Papa."

Entering Prince Roman's and my private apartments, I turned toward the prince's suite, wondering if he were behind the closed doors. A knock and the opening of the main doors caused me to turn.

"Princess Lucille," Lady Buckingham said with a smile. "I'm glad you've returned. Let me help you ready for night. I'll draw a bath."

"Is the prince...have you seen him?"

"No, Your Highness, neither he nor any of his advisors."

As we entered my suite, Lady Buckingham alerted me of my appointment with Mr. Davies. "At ten, following breakfast."

"This is a matter I should discuss with the prince."

"According to Lady Kornhall..."

I wasn't interested in the justification. "Ask her if I could see Mr. Davies earlier. I don't want to miss out on my father's visit."

"Your father?"

"Yes, he will arrive tomorrow morning."

"Your Highness, the senator isn't on tomorrow's approved schedule."

"Then add him."

Lady Buckingham nodded. "I will suggest—"

"Add him," I said with more conviction than normal. "And move my appointment to eight."

"Yes, Your Highness."

CHAPTER 22

Lucille

Awakened and dressed much earlier than usual, I was sitting at the window in my private parlor, sipping tea and eating fruit with toast and jam when the door to the parlor opened.

Roman's laser-focused stare met mine as he closed the door behind him.

"Your Highness," I said, standing, and followed with a curtsy.

His deep voice was lowered. "I'm sorry I didn't make it to the gazebo last night."

"I told you not to apologize."

He reached for my hands. "We're in private."

"Are you sure it's safe?"

Roman tugged me toward my bedchamber. My suite was the same as his, only reversed. It wasn't odd that he would know the way. Once inside, he again closed the door to the outer parlor. "I don't know anymore. I'd hope the Firm would respect the privacy of one's bedchamber." His dark eyes opened wide. "I wanted to talk more before this morning's guest arrives. Are you ready for today's meeting with your father?"

"Yes, I think. Well, after my appointment with Mr. Davies."

Roman's gaze narrowed. "The royal physician. Are you ill?"

"No." Taking a step away, I turned toward the wall and looked up at the portrait of Theodore Rothiford Godfrey IV in a white gown. All I'd been told was that Prince Theodore was King Theodore and Queen Anne's first son, who was tragically lost in an accident when he was an infant.

I turned as Roman's hand came gently to my shoulder. "I wasn't told."

My gaze met his. "It's the same reason I am constantly examined. Mr. Davies and you have apparently discussed trying IUI to improve my chances of conceiving."

"IUI?"

"Intrauterine insemination."

His dark eyes closed with a huff.

"Roman?"

"It has not been discussed with me. And in my opinion, the last thing you want is to bring an heir into this circus."

"But you're here to make things better."

"And where will they get the sperm?"

I hadn't thought of that. "Roman, I presume." My chin fell to my chest. "This is an uncomfortable discussion."

With his thumb and forefinger, Roman lifted my gaze to his. "I don't mean to make you uncomfortable, Lucille. I'm concerned."

"Where were you last night?" I asked.

"The classified information I'm able to access must be done with a deputy of the ministry present. Last night, after you left the dining room, I was summoned to my office by the chief minister. She showed me some recently discovered documents that may help with today's meeting."

"With my father?"

"Yes."

"Is it anything I should know...to help me?" I asked.

Roman exhaled as he took a step back. "You shouldn't know this."

"Would it help if I did?"

"It is believed that your father proposed that in the new agreement the US would pay exactly the same as they had for the last seven years, appeasing the budget concerns."

"Is that good or bad?"

"It's not good, but also not bad. The less favorable part of his proposal is a suggestion that Molave increases exports by twenty percent per year, exclusively to the US."

"Pay the same," I said, "and receive more." My eyes opened wide. "I remember Roman being upset that the resources were losing value." I had an idea. "Is this enough information for you to successfully communicate with my father?"

"Potentially. However, I'd like you to try as we planned. My gut is telling me there is more that I should know. Why would the king press this agreement if he had this information? He knows who I am. Does he not want me to succeed?"

I lifted my hand to his cleanly shaved cheek. "You will succeed."

Taking my hand, Roman kissed my palm.

"I'll do what I can."

"Cancel the medical appointment," Roman said. "Tell them I forbid it."

"You would not, Your Highness."

His smile grew. "Tell them you will conceive the old-fashioned way."

Warmth filled my cheeks. "So far, that hasn't worked. I had the appointment moved to eight." I looked down at my watch. "Soon. I will be back here before nine."

"I'll escort Senator Sutton to our private apartment."

"I cannot bring him into my bedchamber."

Roman nodded. "Perhaps a stroll? The sun is mercifully shining today."

"Molavian winters are dark."

"It gets worse?" he asked with a smile.

"Much worse." I knew my time was limited. "Roman, the king spoke to me last night. He appeared while I was in the gazebo. He asked about you." Being perfectly transparent with this man was easier than it should be. There was his familiarity as well as his improved personality.

The tiny fissures of worry formed near Roman's dark eyes. "What about me?"

"He asked how you seemed. I told him the same, that we rarely speak. However, I did let it slip that I knew my father would arrive in the morning."

Roman's nostrils flared. "That can be explained."

"I did. I hope. I told him you were pacifying me. I'd made my displeasure known that any trip to America would be delayed."

He nodded. "Very good."

There was a knock and we both turned toward the opening door.

"Leave us," Roman bellowed a millisecond after Lady Buckingham's gaze went to both of us.

"Your Highnesses..." Her voice trailed away as the door closed.

"I must go," I said, looking at my watch.

Roman reached for my hand. "Will they complete the procedure today?"

"It's not the right time," I said, looking down.

"Good."

My lips curled as I glanced upward. "Why do you care?"

"I don't know, Lucille. I should have walked away. I should be on a beach in sunny Southern California. I'm a foreigner here but know that I do care. I want to concentrate on the senator, but now I'm concerned about your appointment."

"Don't be. I've had more examinations in the last four and a half years than in my entire life. Mostly, this subject upsets you."

He grinned. "Of course it does. Everything does." He lifted my hand to his firm lips, brushing my knuckles with a soft kiss. "Come to my offices once you're done. I'll inform Lady Buckingham."

* * *

Following my examination, I dressed and waited for the chief royal physician. Five steps one direction and four the other. I paced the small room. Finally, the knock came to the door.

"Come in," I commanded, standing tall as Mr. Davies entered.

"Your Highness, we have confirmed that you're not currently with child."

I didn't think I was pregnant; nevertheless, the verification never came as a relief.

"Based on your menstruation..." Mr. Davies went on to explain the timing of the procedure and what was involved.

"And you're certain the prince approves?" I asked.

"While he should have told you that himself, yes. The procedure has reached the highest level of approval."

Highest level—King Theodore.

The doctor went on, "Use the app the nurse installed on your phone and record your temperature every morning upon waking. In ten days, we will complete the procedure. However, if it doesn't succeed the first time, the information we're gathering through the app will help us the following month."

"Thank you, Doctor."

"And one more thing."

"Yes."

"The prince will be informed that during this

period as your body prepares for fertilization, no intercourse."

My lips came together at the realization. This wasn't as much about the IUI as it was preventing Roman—the new Roman—and me from having sex.

Did someone know about the act we gave Lady Buckingham yesterday?

That question and others swirled through my thoughts as I left the exam room. I met Lady Buckingham waiting outside the infirmary. Her gray gaze met mine with a smile and curtsy. As we made our way through the palace toward Roman's offices, I questioned the woman at my side, wondering who I could trust, indeed if there was anyone.

When we reached the official offices of the crown prince of Molave, the guard outside the door granted us passage with a bow after addressing me with the usual title. I'd expected to wait or to go into one of the many rooms within the office suite. Instead, my father was seated on a sofa with a cup of tea at his side.

As the secretaries who were present stood and curtsied, my father's blue eyes opened wide as I came into his view.

With a grin, he stood, bowed his head, and looked up, his smile even larger. "Lucille."

Forgetting about the audience, I hurried to his

arms. Relief and comfort flooded my circulation as he held me in an embrace.

When I pulled away, I took a step back, the excitement in my voice impossible to disguise. "Dad, I just learned you were to be here." I looked around. "Where is Roman? How is Mom? Why couldn't she come along?"

CHAPTER 23

Lucille

"The prince was called away as soon as I arrived," my dad said with a slight smile. He patted my hand now on his arm. "It's a welcome surprise that I get to visit with the princess."

I looked around at our audience. "Come, the sun is shining. A rarity this time of year in Molave City. We can take a walk."

He looked concerned.

I spoke to one of the secretaries. "Miss Park."

The young lady stood. "Inform the prince that Senator Sutton is with me in the gardens. I'll return the senator," I said with a grin toward my father, "when the prince returns."

"Your Highness," Miss Park said with a curtsy.

Leading my father through the palace, we finally came to one of the many sets of French doors that led out into the gardens. It was the first time in a while I'd been out along the paths in the daylight. High above us the sky was a soft blue with light wisps of clouds. A chilled breeze blew rogue strands of dark hair around my face.

"How are you?" I asked, still holding to his arm.

"I'm well." My father's expression morphed from happy to unease. "Lucy, how are you? Your mother and I are concerned."

"I'm well. Why are you concerned?"

"The unrest last month was all over the news in the States. There have been reports of disagreements between the king and your husband. And now there are issues with what I believed settled. It's a matter of state."

"Between the US and Molave?" I asked.

"It's why I'm here. Your mother didn't know we'd be granted an audience." His smile warmed me from the inside. "She will be pleased as well as sad."

"Tell her I miss her."

"I will."

We were deep into the center of the gardens when I began Roman's plan. "Roman has finally given me permission to help with matters of state." I sighed. "He doesn't think I'll succeed. That's why he gave me the go-ahead to speak to you. He assumes that if I make a blithering idiot out of myself, my secret will be safe with you. You won't run to the press or the king."

Dad stopped walking and looked down at me. "Is it true the prince fears King Theodore?"

I took half a step back. "No, King Theo is...he is no one to fear."

With his lips together, Dad nodded. "It goes against my better judgment to include you in these matters."

"Because I'm your daughter instead of a son?"

"Lucille, never has your gender been a negative. You are you, and your mother and I couldn't love or respect you more. I'm uneasy because we worry about your safety. I promised your mother if by some miracle, I had the chance to talk to you privately, I'd ask you a question."

My pulse kicked up a notch as I looked around. There was no guarantee we weren't being watched from one of the windows on the second or third floor, yet as for close to us, no one was near enough to overhear. "Ask."

"Have you considered divorce?"

My eyes opened wide. "Why would Mom ever want you to ask that?"

"She worries that when you two speak, your conversations aren't private. She's concerned you aren't speaking freely." He smiled a sad smile. "She's your mother, and she's worried about you. If divorce and returning home are things you've been considering, we will support you. It would be easier before you and Roman have a child."

My chin lowered. "That's not happening, not yet."

"Good. I'll promise the support of the US embassy in returning you safely to the US if you would ask."

I shook my head. "I'm not considering it," I said honestly. "I have more hope for Molave than I've had in a long time. With this" —I motioned between us— "as a test run, I am hopeful that Roman is serious about allowing me a more active role as princess. I took a vow."

"There are rumors about Borinkia. As your mother's daughter, you would not be safe."

"As the princess of Molave, I would."

Dad leaned his forehead down to mine and spoke softly. "If you need our help, tell your mother that you miss her peach pie."

I grinned. "Mom's never made a peach pie in her life."

"She came up with the phrase."

"Just like our fake names at the homeless shelter."

Dad nodded. "Say the phrase and I will immediately contact the embassy." He inhaled. "What has Roman shared about the arrangement between Molave and the US?"

"Not much. I believe he wants to find out if I can learn details on my own." When I met Dad's gaze, I feigned a grin. "There are a lot of tests in my position."

"In every position, sweetheart. Life is a constant

test. Your mother and I don't want you spending the rest of yours regretting your decision or feeling there are no options."

"For once," I said, resuming our slow pace, "I am excited about the options."

"Do you know about Greenland?" he asked.

I nodded.

"My obvious connection to Molave will be questioned by the House Ethics Committee," Dad said. "To lessen that speculation with the prospect of obtaining natural resources from Greenland, I made a reasonable proposal to the prince."

"And he wasn't happy."

"Enraged may be a better word. I thought it would go more smoothly. It's why I arranged to come here."

"The same money with a yearly increase in exports," I said, hoping Roman had been informed right.

"Twenty percent," Dad said.

"Were there other stipulations?"

"Roman wanted increased payment without the increase in exports."

I met my father's gaze. "I cannot make deals. Theoretically, they all must go through the king and Parliament."

"Soon, Roman will have that crown."

I tilted my head. "King Theodore is well. I spoke with him last night."

"I was told..." Dad shook his head. "How about we walk and you tell me what you've been doing to stay busy?"

"What were you told?" I asked.

"Sweetheart, I want to spend this rare opportunity with my daughter talking about something other than the king of Molave."

Placing my hand back in the crook of his arm, we resumed our stroll. As I told my father about life at Annabella Castle, I did my best to embellish the day-to-day routine. I put emphasis on my gardens and preparing for the upcoming winter. I even mentioned that Roman and I may be approved for a North American tour after the first of the year.

Those were the things we were discussing when Lord Martin met us.

"Your Highness." He bowed. "Mr. Sutton, the prince apologizes for the interruption. He's now in his office, awaiting your arrival."

As Lord Martin hurried ahead, Dad whispered, "Do you think he apologized?"

My lips curled into a grin. "I doubt it."

Dad patted my hand.

A few minutes later, Roman's voice boomed from his inner office.

"Send them in."

The sharpness of his tone combined with the volume truly sent off the same nonverbal responses the real Roman could induce: an increase in pulse rate, a chill over my skin, and perspiration to my palms.

"You'll be going?" Dad asked.

"After I'm dismissed by my husband."

Dad snickered. "The first time I dismiss the baroness you will learn of my demise."

"This is an odd world," I said, repeating the impostor's words. "And a real world. Things are different in public."

"Duchess," Roman said with a scowl as I entered with my father.

"Your Highness." I completed the customary curtsy. "I'm simply delivering my father. Thank you for allowing us time to see one another."

Roman waved his hand. "My schedule is..." He shook his head before standing.

Dad bowed his head before going forward and shaking Roman's hand. No one in Molave shook the prince's hand. I supposed my father's status as both Roman's father-in-law and a representative of the United States called for different protocol.

"We have business, Lucille," Roman said dismissively.

"And I will leave you to it." My gaze met Roman's

as I nodded. "My meeting with the royal physician was a success. While it riled him, it was exactly as he'd said."

Roman let out a breath. "We will talk later."

I bowed my head before going to my father. "Tell Mother I love her and miss her."

He reached for my hand. "Physician? Are you ill?"

"No, Dad. Routine."

His expression morphed. "He was riled?"

Smiling my biggest smile, I squeezed his hand. "All is well. I promise. Tell Mom."

"That you miss her cooking?" he asked with a weary smile.

"No. Her and you. Once I know more about the North American tour, I will let you know."

"Take care, dear."

"I will, Dad." With that, I left a kiss on his cheek and a final glance at my husband.

Despite the performance, I saw a bit of relief in Roman's expression, the way his chiseled jaw was no longer clenched and the easing of the worry lines near his eyes. Leaving Roman's office, I had the undeniable sensation that I'd helped...in a minor way. I hoped I did.

My thoughts returned to who I could trust.

My father.

I could trust my father.

CHAPTER 24

Oliver

"He thinks you're a pompous ass." Lucille's assessment came back to me as I gestured for Edwin Sutton to take the seat opposite my desk.

"Your Highness," the senator said. His eyes, the color of his daughter's, were upon me. "My delegation is headed on to Sweden later today. I wish I'd been able to schedule more time."

Inhaling, I sat back, undid the front buttons of my suitcoat and stared at my father-in-law. "The original agreement isn't due to expire—"

"As I told you, Borinkia has asked for an audience."

"It is against our treaty for the US to negotiate with Borinkia."

"There are many members of the Senate who want to do away with the old treaty."

Edwin Sutton and I went back and forth in an even exchange.

From the crumbs Lucille left, I believed the information Mrs. Drake had shared last evening was accurate. The senator wanted an agreement that would pay Molave the same amount as last time with a twenty-percent increase in exports each year for seven more years. As our negotiation continued, I released enough information to receive more.

The senator spoke of compromises and possible obstruction.

While I'd never concerned myself too much with American politics, I was certain I understood the subject better than the real Roman Godfrey. When I'd had enough, I stood. "It's your concern when dealing with the necessary votes. However, keep in mind that Molave will consider any American negotiation with Borinkia an act of aggression."

"And what of your negotiation with Prince Volkov?" Senator Sutton asked.

I knew of rumors, but as with this particular agreement, Roman hadn't left anything in the way of notes or documentation. "That is not your concern."

"It is, Your Highness, because of my daughter. My wife, Lucille's mother, was born in Letanonia..."

I nodded dismissively. "As the princess of Molave, your daughter's safety is an utmost concern."

"I hope to God you're telling me the truth."

"What rumors have you heard?" I asked, trying not to sound as curious as I actually was.

"Volkov has a sister," the senator said with a grimace. "Combining the two monarchies, increasing landmass, resources, citizens, and Borinkia has a stronger army."

A sister.

I would need to investigate.

Surely, he wasn't insinuating that I would take a new wife.

Ignoring my gut reaction, I said, "Molave is a peaceful state."

"Their army is larger."

And we had more financial resources.

"What you speak of," I said, "is not within my power."

"Once King Theodore is gone, it will be. And then what of Lucille?"

Looking him in the eye, I swore another oath. "Your daughter is safe with me."

"You've told me that before."

"Then there should be no reason to repeat myself," I said, my volume raising. "I will take your proposal to my father; however, I will change twenty to ten. A ten-percent increase in exports each year and an increase from fifteen to twenty billion paid up front for our guarantee of exports."

"I knew your earlier offer was too good to be true."

"It was your proposal. Not my offer." Buttoning my

jacket, I smiled. "Take that offer to your colleagues and not only will our countries remain allies, but you have my solemn promise that Lucille will remain safe."

"Word is that you're not to be trusted."

I stood tall and squared my shoulders. "You're fortunate that I love your daughter. Otherwise, I would take that as an insult."

"That is the first time I've heard those words from your lips."

"I take insults seriously."

"That you love Lucille," he clarified, his expression softening.

"She is my wife."

The senator nodded. "That I've heard many times."

I pushed the button on the edge of my desk. "Goodbye, Senator. I look forward to hearing from you regarding our agreement."

Before I was done speaking, the door to my office was opened and Lord Martin stood with his hands clasped behind his back. "Your Highness."

"Lord Martin, the senator has an appointment. Please see him to his car."

As the door shut, I let out a long breath and collapsed into my chair.

That went well.

I believe it went well.

My first instinct was to tell Lucille. Alas, she'd have to wait.

I lifted the telephone receiver. When my secretary answered, I said, "Alert the king that I'm available for counsel upon his request."

"Yes, Your Highness."

Later that afternoon, I was the person on the less impressive side of the desk, relaying most of the information I'd received as well as the deal I'd proposed. King Theodore seemed pleased, nodding his agreement as I spoke.

"You received no indication that Edwin questioned your identity?"

"I'm in the palace in Molave City. He came to my office. It's rare for anyone to question what they see with their own eyes and hear with their own ears when the surroundings support that belief. The tougher job will be when I'm out of the palace."

"I agree." He shrugged. "I'm more than pleased with your progress and not only that, but all that you were able to confirm without much information from Roman."

"Have you asked him?"

The king stood and taking a deep breath, walked over to the highboy and poured himself a finger of what appeared to be bourbon. "I'd offer you a glass, but I'm not willing to chance the consequences if you became intoxicated."

"I'm not much of a drinker, Your Majesty. I do enjoy a good bourbon."

"This is scotch," he said, lifting the glass. Taking the rim to his lips, he emptied the tumbler and exhaled. "Superb." His dark gaze met mine. "Have you had any contact with anyone from your old life?"

"Other than Andrew..."

"Andrew?"

"Andrew Briggs, my agent. Mrs. Drake contacted him. It was how I was summoned to Molave." Some instinct told me to keep Dustin Hargraves out of this. The chief minister knew about my agent. "Andrew is the only one who knows where I am."

The king nodded and walked back to his chair. "Don't mention the scotch at dinner. I don't want to deal with Anne."

A grin broke out across my face. "Your secret is safe with me."

"I feel it's time for you to address the citizens of Molave as well as join me at a few upcoming summits. It would be good for you to be both seen and heard. And to still the rumors of my demise." He sat tall. "I'm very much alive."

"What of Princess Lucille?"

He leaned forward. "At this point in our dealings, the less interaction the two of you have, the better."

"It isn't unusual. From all I've been told, they weren't close."

"Shame," the king said with a shake of his head. "He ruined what there once was. In many ways, I believe it is irreparable."

"I was informed" —I didn't say by whom— "that the princess had an appointment with Mr. Davies this morning."

"It isn't your concern."

The small hairs on my arms stood tall. "She's my wife."

"In name only. She has an important role to play and despite the ineptitude of Roman—the other Roman—it's time that she fulfills her obligation."

"Was she asked?"

The king only stared.

"Did anyone ask Lucille if she wanted to fulfill that role?"

"She made a vow, as have you. It's best for you to remain in your own lane, my son."

I'd moved from boy to son.

Having never been close to my own father, it had a nice ring. I had an idea, a place that may allow Lucille and I to speak more freely. "My morning briefings came with news of predicted snow in Monovia. I could accompany the princess to Annabella Castle and return."

"While she's under Mr. Davies's care, she is to remain untouched."

My teeth came together as I wondered if the king was giving me permission to bed his son's wife after she was declared impregnated. Pushing that thought away, I nodded. "I promised the senator that Lucille would stay safe. It is simply a fulfillment of my promise, a good faith measure. When Lucille mentions it to her parents, it will aid in the sincerity of our proposal."

The king nodded. "Tomorrow. And then return, post haste. We have much work to do before the Group of Fifteen Eurasia summit."

"Thank you, Your Majesty."

He shook his head. "Someone instilled too many manners in you, son. You're a prince. You have no one to thank, not even me."

"My mother," I said with a grin, "I'd assume."

"She overdid herself." His gaze narrowed. "Where does she believe you are?"

"I'd assume she knows."

"Do we have her contact information?"

"She's gone, Your Grace. My mother's knowledge would come from the afterworld. I'm not sure there is one, but if there is, she deserves to be there."

"Very well. I should have known Mrs. Drake

would have all bases covered." He waved his hand. "I will see you at dinner. Be sure to tell your mother you're accompanying the princess to Annabella Castle. She'll be happy for days." He wasn't speaking of the woman who birthed and raised me but of the queen.

"The queen is unaware of Lucille's upcoming procedure?" I asked.

"You should not be aware."

"My briefings, sir. They're thorough."

"The queen is happy to be less informed."

CHAPTER 25

Lucille

I'd been elated when Lady Buckingham informed me that Prince Roman would accompany me to Annabella. Of course, I couldn't act as if I were excited. Yet in my mind, I imagined showing him around the castle. In all our years of marriage, I'd never been the one to inform Roman of anything. This new paradigm was enticing.

That delight waned when Lady Buckingham entered the back seat, sitting at my side.

"The prince?" I asked.

"He's riding with Lord Martin and Lord Taylor, Your Highness."

I feigned a smile. "Then we shall have a relaxing ride."

She lowered her voice, looking straight ahead. "Then perhaps I should not tell you of another search?"

Following her cue, I remained poised with my voice a bit over a whisper. "Another, of Annabella?"

Lady Buckingham nodded.

"The royal guards?"

"No, same as before, deputies of the ministry."

"Has this happened before and I was simply unaware?"

"Not to my knowledge, Your Highness. Although they explained to Mrs. Templeton that it was routine."

It had to be about the new Roman.

For the next hour, my prophecy of a relaxing and even thought-provoking ride held true. It was as the royal fleet climbed the mountainous roads, clouds descended, and the snow fell in earnest that I became increasingly concerned. "Perhaps we should turn around and head back to Molave City?" I asked the royal guard driving our car.

"The prince instructed us to carry on, Your Highness."

I reached for Lady Buckingham's hand as visibility beyond the windshield decreased, and our tires intermittently lost traction. The vehicle's speed slowed as the roads became indistinguishable from the landscape. If I didn't know the terrain I wouldn't be as upset.

I did know the terrain.

There were curves with nothing more than cliffs on the other side.

My head pounded as I clenched my teeth and closed my eyes. The muscles in my neck and shoulders tensed as I anticipated falling to our deaths. I wanted to question the prince myself but doing so would be out of character. The thing was, *this* Roman wasn't familiar with the terrain of Monovia. He may have read about it or looked at maps. That didn't compare to the reality that we were teetering on slick precipices that could end the concerns about the monarchy or the future king.

One wrong move and one or all of our vehicles could plummet to the depths, leaving Isabella to rule Molave.

While the king's decree of my IUI didn't feel right, I wasn't ready to die. Watching the blowing snow beyond the windows of the car, I imagined a child of my own or maybe two. I entertained thoughts of Rothy and Alice. I mourned the hopes I'd allowed to bud and grow within me of Molave and of making a difference.

It wasn't until we neared the castle that I remembered to breathe with a normal rhythm. The blue sky from earlier in Molave City was no longer visible, replaced by a fog of snow and condensation. We traveled within those clouds covering the mountains. The rural landscape of Monovia was covered in a blanket of white with more snow accumulating.

We passed through the first gate to Annabella approximately four hours after leaving the palace in Molave City. That was twice the time the trip usually took. By the time the fleet pulled up to the castle and came to a stop beneath the arch, I was both tired and upset. It would have been easy for Roman to tell the guards to return to Molave City. If only I could have spoken to him.

Once my door was opened, my fantasies of taking Roman on a tour were gone.

The castle staff stood outside the doors. Despite the frigid temperatures, they lined up beneath the stone arch protecting us from direct snow. Each person bowed and offered greetings as I stalked past. Once inside, I removed my gloves and long wool coat, handed them to Lady Buckingham, and gave a strict order. "I'm not to be disturbed."

"Dinner, Your Highness."

I spun toward her. "Leave it in the connected parlor."

Connected.

I turned as Prince Roman entered with a dusting of snow and a gust of cold air.

"Princess."

I didn't notice his slight smile or the way his dark eyes glistened under the light of the large chandelier. My thoughts were too focused on what we'd all endured.

"We could have died," I said too loudly and force-fully. "These roads. You don't know how dangerous..."

Roman's eyes opened wide as his deep voice boomed through the cavernous foyer. "I don't know my own kingdom? Do not speak to me in such a tone."

The eyes of all those around us were on us. Once more, I hadn't been thinking. I'd been too concerned for our survival.

Gritting my teeth, I curtsied. "I apologize, Your Highness. I'll be retiring. I'm not well."

"We are not done." He turned to his advisors. "The roads are unsafe. You'll spend the night here."

"I'll make up your rooms," Mrs. Templeton, the head of housekeeping, said to the men.

I only briefly met Roman's gaze before taking off to our private apartments and leaving the voices behind me.

My mind was a cyclone of thoughts. Our lives were still intact, and yet I jeopardized them with my words in front of Lord Martin and Lord Taylor as well as the Annabella staff. It was the second time I'd almost ruined Roman's role. First with the king and now here.

When I'd first learned of the impostor, I truly believed I could carry on this charade, but perhaps I couldn't. My father's offer to help me divorce came to mind. If the new Roman was the answer to Molave's future, perhaps it would be better if I weren't at his side.

Is it really a divorce if the man you are married to isn't the man you married?

With my temples thumping, I entered our private apartments and turned left toward my suite. I was barely inside when I heard the heavy pounding of the footsteps behind me. Spinning, I pushed to close the door.

My efforts proved fruitless as Roman placed his shoe in the doorjamb.

"I'm sorry, Lucille. I didn't realize."

"Stop apologizing," I said, my emotions winning as tears streamed down my cheeks.

"Lord Taylor was filling me in on the upcoming summit. I wasn't paying attention."

How could he not see our peril?

I lowered my voice. "Does Lord Taylor know about you?"

Roman shook his head.

"Lord Martin?"

"Yes. He's been on my team since the first day of my arrival."

Wrapping my arms around my midsection, I took a deep breath and nodded. "What has become of Lord Avery?"

"I don't know that name."

"He was Roman's...Lord Martin, his chief assistant."

"Maybe he's with Roman."

My gaze met Roman's. "I was afraid," I admitted. "So very scared, more so than I recall ever being. I don't want to die. I don't want you to die...Lady Buckingham." My body trembled as I continued. "And downstairs, I spoke without thinking, which is also dangerous. I don't want to ruin everything for you."

"We're in this together."

I shook my head. "It's so much. Too much."

"I was wrong."

For a moment, I stared. "I'm not used to hearing you admitting that."

Roman's dark eyes shone as he bowed his head and again met my gaze. "I was raised with manners, Princess. It goes against my upbringing to forget that." He reached out, caressing my cheek with his thumb. "I was wrong about the drive and involving you in this charade."

"I..." My reply faded away as Roman looked over his shoulder to the empty large room, confirming our privacy.

Lady Buckingham had minded my warning, allowing me space.

My heart skipped a beat as Roman took a step toward me.

One step backward and he followed until we were both within my parlor. Quietly, he closed the door behind him. "As long as I'm around, you don't have to be frightened alone." He lifted his arms.

Against all better judgment, I took a step toward Roman and leaned into him as his arms surrounded me. My cheek settled upon his chest, cushioned by the padded shirt beneath, as the faint thump of his heart sounded in my ear. Closing my eyes, the rich scent of his cologne surrounded me as I gave into the emotions I'd worked for years to keep closed away.

Roman's touch started as comforting circles on my back. Slowly, the circles moved lower as his other hand found its way to my neck.

Without thinking, I lifted my tearstained face to his, where without hesitation our lips connected. Unlike the passionate kisses or even the timid kisses, this one was different. It warmed me from within while cementing a bond we had no right to pursue.

Together.

We were in this together.

Roman's hand came to my cheek. "I vowed to keep you safe, and I've already failed."

"No, I'm safe. We're here."

He looked around and grinned. "Our home."

"Our castle. It's never been much of a home."

His forehead fell to mine. "Tonight, I'll send for you."

"I cannot. Mr. Davies..."

Roman smirked. "I've been told."

"I have to wonder if it's the king's way of protecting me."

"You're safe with me, Princess. I'd simply like to talk. By morning, you'll be back in your own bedchamber. Now, I must go down to my offices and continue my work with Lord Taylor and Lord Martin."

"Do you know where to go?"

He smiled. "I've studied the blueprints."

"Of course you have. I wanted to take you on a tour."

"Rest and please eat. Tonight, I'll not stand you up."

I shrugged. "King Theo filled in for you."

"Not tonight."

CHAPTER 26

Oliver

As an actor by profession, I'd become adept at staging, knowing where to stand and toward what direction to speak. On the stage, the same space could morph into multiple settings. In the opening scene we could appear to be walking on a street in New York, the Empire State Building glowing in the background. That was all it took, one instantly recognizable element to transport the audience without a verbal cue.

The universe where I was the warlord far outspent the budgets of Broadway. Our sets were both within the confines of the sound studios as well as throughout the world. Taking their cues from other successful enterprises, we shot scenes in castles in Scotland as well as remote beaches in the south of France.

The script was key.

A good script was more than words. It gave instructions and cues that the director could or would change on impulse. The trick was to learn all the information in the script and be adaptable to the whims of the directors or producers.

It was also the people behind the scenes, the CGI specialists, those who worked their magic on computers and coordinating sound, and even the costume design and makeup artists whose talents truly created the production that viewers saw.

As I traversed the hallways of Annabella Castle, I longed to slow and take in my surroundings. There was history in the artwork. I'd read about much of it, but being within the corridors was the next step, the bigger budget. Yet there was no time to soak in what was Roman's home.

My costume was intact, and I had been given the script, yet as I approached the offices, I needed to rely upon my ability to adapt. Lord Martin would not stay in attendance. As my personal assistant he wasn't involved in the matters of state as was Lord Taylor, a royal minister charged with foreign affairs.

Lord Martin was more than my assistant. He was my current director, informing me of my blocking—where I should stand and move—and dialogue. There was an almost frightening sensation when I was left to my own devices. It was a narrow road, a tightrope, that kept others believing and the real me from taking over.

And still, in all scenes, the premise of Roman Godfrey needed to remain believable. Not only was

Lord Taylor my audience, but the rest of the Annabella Castle staff and Lady Buckingham were too. The only greenroom or trailer, so to speak—a place to rehearse and regroup—was the privacy of my own bedchamber.

For only a moment, I thought about the promise I'd made to Lucille, telling her I would call for her. As I nodded at the royal guard outside my office suites, I tucked my thoughts of the princess away and revived the ruthless monarch I was meant to be.

"Your Royal Highness," everyone within the office said with a bow or a curtsy.

"Lord Taylor," I commanded. "Come into my office, and we will continue the conversation."

"Your Highness, if I may," Lord Martin said.

"Go on," I gestured for Lord Taylor to enter the next room. It was customary for me to be first to enter unless instructed otherwise. The office contained information that should not be available to others without me present.

Since I'd never entered these office suites, I wasn't aware of what was within. That was for me to learn. Lifting my chin, I wordlessly instructed the others present to leave us.

"On with it," I said, once Lord Martin and I were alone.

"The princess?"

"What of her?"

"Does she know?" Lord Martin asked, his volume lower.

Lying wasn't my go-to; however, if protecting Lucille was my goal, exposing her knowledge would only be a liability to us both. "Know what?"

He lowered his voice. "Your identity, sir. The way she spoke to you..." He shook his head. "I've never before heard Princess Lucille raise her voice."

"The princess was upset. She's upstairs in her suite morbidly reliving what she was sure was to be our deaths."

"And you comforted her?"

Irritation at his line of questioning skirted my flesh in the same way an un-scratchable itch would. My volume rose. "What occurs between the princess and me is not your concern. I'll not be questioned about it again."

Lord Martin bowed his head. "I apologize, Your Highness. Your success is my success. Not that I advocate for maintaining the strain of your relationship; however, in the past you would have been more forceful regarding her outburst."

"You just said she never had an outburst."

He nodded. "If she had."

"In front of staff and cabinet ministers?"

"In private, sir."

"I handled it." It was the line I'd been told to use from my first interaction with the royal family.

Lord Martin nodded. "Very well. I've recently..." He lifted his chin. "There has been mention that if the princess's upcoming procedure is unsuccessful, that perhaps you and the princess will agree to divorce."

"What?"

"It would be easier to maintain the persona with a new bride. There is the princess of Borinkia."

I shook my head, lowered my volume, and stalked toward my assistant. "You're springing this on me now?" My question came out more as the growl I was feeling.

Lord Martin held his ground. "The king is in negotiations. I was only recently made aware."

"Made aware? You were not officially informed?" I was beginning to understand the code of this crazy world.

"Correct."

I recalled Senator Sutton mentioning Prince Volkov's sister.

"I need to know what is being discussed," I said. "Bring me everything, whether it's official or not. If there are rumors, then someone is talking."

Lord Martin nodded.

"Send the secretaries back in," I commanded. "I'll

be with Lord Taylor until evening meal. That I'll take upstairs with the princess."

"Alone?"

"Yes, she's recuperating."

With a smile, Lord Martin nodded. "Very good, sir."

Heat boiled beneath my clothing at Lord Martin's approval of Roman's relationship with Princess Lucille. He'd said more forceful. The most forceful I would ever be was what transpired in the foyer. Lucille's recuperation was from her onset of nerves brought on by the driving conditions, not because I handled her obstinance in a physical manner.

Opening the door to my office, I met Lord Taylor's gaze as he stood and bowed. Much like the offices in the palace in Molave City, the room was tall with tapestries and bookcases, an ostentatious large desk, a conference table, and a corner reserved for sofas and more comfortable chairs. Beyond the large windows, the snow continued to fall and swirl in miniature cyclones.

"Your Highness," the foreign-affairs minister said, gesturing over folders of documents. "As you know, the other governments present at the Group of Fifteen Eurasia Summit are..."

I did my best to equal parts listen and learn, but at the same time, I grew increasingly impatient. It wasn't difficult to let my thoughts wander if I went back to what Lord Martin had said.

Divorce.

To continue this role without Lucille was not in my plans. However, as Lord Taylor droned on endlessly about alliances and the importance of appearance, I came to the realization that my vow was never to Lucille but to the crown and Molave.

I couldn't fathom one without the other.

"Your Highness?" Lord Taylor asked, pulling me from my thoughts.

"I'm bored." It wasn't meant to be in character, just an honest moment in a foreign voice.

Lord Taylor sat back and smiled.

"Is that amusing?" I asked, standing and walking to the windows. Despite it only being near five o'clock, the storm brought an earlier-than-usual darkness with the continued accumulation.

"I was concerned, Your Highness."

"Are you questioning my health, sir, or my ability?"

"Neither," he said with a shake of his head. "We can resume this review tomorrow." He nodded toward the window. "I'm afraid returning to Molave City won't be prudent for a day or two."

"Papa thinks I'm incapable." It was the excuse bestowed upon Lord Taylor for the reason I was in need of this advanced information on the fifteen country states that would be present at the upcoming summit.

"I believe, sir, the king wants to be certain you understand Molave's historic stance."

"Why would I not?"

"The last summit, sir, as well as the recent tour..."

He wasn't saying that they went poorly, but from what I'd gleaned, those public events had gone horribly. Of course, I wasn't Roman Godfrey during those times, not that Lord Taylor was privy to that information.

I waved the foreign-affairs minister away. "Tomorrow."

Lord Taylor bowed. "Your Highness."

After he was gone, the door opened with a knock.

"Yes, yes," I said, staring out the window, expecting Lord Martin.

"Your Highness."

I spun around to the most stunning blue stare. "Princess."

She curtsied. "I came to apologize for my outburst this afternoon."

"It is I..." My words trailed away at the sight of her widening eyes and shaking head. "Close the door," I said with more force.

After she did as I instructed, we both stood for a moment in silence. The bodice of her jumper stretched with each of her breaths as her breasts pushed against the fabric. As her pink lips curled, I moved toward her. Meeting in the middle of the room, I reached for her hands and kept my volume low. "What is it?"

"A feeling. I'll explain tonight."

"About?" I prompted.

"Lady Buckingham has confided in me that deputies from the ministry have been here at Annabella Castle twice recently, both times while I was called away."

My pulse increased. "Deputies? In what capacity?"

"Searching is all she's been told. I assume it has to do with you."

"I've never been here before."

"No, Your Highness, Roman." She turned toward one of the bookcases. Moving closer, she ran the tips of her fingers over the spines. "King Theo asked me if you kept journals, saying that some rulers think themselves self-important and therefore have a need to record their daily activities."

Going closer, I laid my hand on her slender shoulder. Lucille's beautiful blue orbs looked up at me. "Did I?" I asked.

"Not to my knowledge." She exhaled. "I should go."

"We will dine alone in our parlor."

"Please, Roman, don't trust the parlor. Our

bedchambers are the only places we can talk freely. I've never worried about this before, but now..." She nodded. "I feel a shift. Things are different."

Things were different because I'd involved Lucille in the deception. Her unease was my doing, causing my insides to stir with concern. Focusing only on her, I nodded.

"Again, Your Highness, I am sorry."

My volume rose. "As long as you know your duty..." Yes, it was a speech I knew and detested at the same time. "And inform Lady Buckingham that after dinner and your bath, you are to come to my suite."

Lucille curtsied, keeping her gorgeous blue gaze veiled. "Yes, Your Highness."

CHAPTER
27

Lucille

"The royal physician advised..." Lady Buckingham said, turning toward me as she poured bath oils into the filling tub.

"I am aware of what Mr. Davies said. He also said the prince was told. Do you suggest I refuse my husband's summons?" I never had, nor had my mistress encouraged such behavior in the past.

"No, Your Highness. Perhaps you can remind him."

Wrapped only in a dressing gown with my long hair piled upon my head, I turned away from my mistress as the remodeled bathroom filled with lilac-scented humidity, and the clawfoot tub reached its proper depth. "I'm certain Roman knows of the physician's orders. He would not appreciate me reminding him." That was true of the old Roman.

"Ma'am?"

Turning back, I stepped closer and untied the sash.

The soft material slid from my shoulders leaving me naked as I reached for Lady Buckingham's hand and stepped into the tub. Lowering myself to the depths, the warm water sloshed and my skin pinkened. My mistress gently ran a loofah over my shoulders and back.

"The weather report is cautioning that up to two meters of snow could fall in the higher elevations..." Lady Buckingham continued speaking as my thoughts circled back to this evening.

I'd felt the urge to warn Roman about the searches. I planned to learn more myself from the house staff. Roman wouldn't be the one to question the maids. That would be me. I'd hoped that making an apology outside of our private apartments would further *this* Roman's believability. Or to those in the know, it would perpetuate my lack of knowledge. With each passing encounter, it was becoming more difficult for me to separate the two men.

Perhaps I didn't want them separated.

I wanted the combination, the man I married and the man this Roman was.

After I was dried and again covered by my dressing gown, Lady Buckingham brushed my dark hair until it fell in soft ringlets she formed around her fingers. I was without makeup, but as I stared at my reflection, I didn't feel the need to enhance my appearance as I might have done for my husband. There was a comfort in this Roman's approval.

It wasn't superficial or expected.

He could easily carry on the behavior of the man he pretended to be, and yet he hadn't.

"No," I said as my mistress reached for the powder. When her gaze came to me, I grinned. "I'm tired from our drive. Let the prince see that."

"A little pink for your lips?"

I shook my head.

"Perhaps he too is tired," she suggested.

"One can only hope."

Lady Buckingham held up two nightgowns. Both were floor-length satin and lace. One was white and the other black. It would under normal circumstances be one of my few choices of the night.

"Black with black bloomers," I said.

Although she didn't protest, I was aware that bloomers weren't always worn when I was summoned. That said, the black nightgown was less transparent, and bloomers were...well, appropriate, considering I didn't truly know the man staying on the other side of our private apartments.

After brushing my teeth and drinking a cup of water, the woman in the mirror was ready to face the impostor.

"I will wait for your return," Lady Buckingham

said as we walked toward the doors to the shared parlor. My black nightgown and bloomers were covered by the dressing gown.

"No. We're all tired. You should go to your quarters and rest." I feigned a smile. "Relax, since we weren't able to do that during the drive."

She curtsied. "If you need me..."

I reached for her hand. "You know I will call."

I had. Over the years, I had called.

"Your Highness."

Walking toward Roman's doors was unlike any other time. Despite my mind knowing the truth of his identity—or impostor status—my body and heart were aflutter as they hadn't been since our courtship. The feelings were all too complicated to sort out. *This* Roman was my creation, the unspoken wishes of my heart and soul personified.

Mr. Davies's direction to avoid intercourse had the opposite effect.

I wanted to rebel against the assumptions and duties I'd worked so diligently to uphold. King Theo thought he could control all things. While he did so in a loving and charming way, nevertheless, his influence was invasive to say the least.

My fist went to Roman's door with a light tap-tap.

The door opened inward to Lord Martin. "Your

Royal Highness," he said with a bow. "The prince is waiting."

"Lord Martin."

Unlike Lord Avery before him, Lord Martin appeared less pleased at my arrival. It was probably because he knew the truth, that this wasn't the man I married. Was he upset with Roman for summoning me, would he tell the king, or was he unhappy that I didn't see what was before me?

My stomach twisted as Lord Martin left the suite and I made my way back to the bedchamber. With each step, my heartbeat thumped in double time in my ears. The small hairs on my arms stood like tiny lightning rods warning of an impending storm.

In my mind, the two men were melding.

The familiar dread threatened my conjured husband.

By the time I lifted my hand to knock on the door to the bedchamber, the hallway around me wavered as if I were seeing it through the distortion of heatwaves. Beneath my dressing gown, my skin grew tight as my temperature rose and my circulation slowed. The door opened as the image of Roman's smile paled, and the world went black.

My eyes blinked as I woke to the sound of breathing and a thumping in my temples. Illumination penetrated the darkness behind my closed lids as I squinted, seeing my own bedchamber around me. My stomach twisted painfully as I tried to make sense of what had occurred.

Closing my eyes, the memories returned.

I'd been summoned.

I was knocking on the door.

Something had happened.

Sitting up with a start, I looked around, searching for a sign that I wasn't mad. That my world was really upside down. My heart rate still felt too rapid as if I had run a race.

"Oh," I exclaimed.

The connection to my dilemma was beside me, lying on top of the blankets, wearing the bottoms to his customary pajamas and no shirt. As I stared at the entirety of him, there was no doubt this impostor was not my husband—not the *real* Roman. This man's cheeks were covered with a day's stubble, and his strong, firm lips were parted. My gaze slowly studied his torso and shoulders no longer hidden beneath a padded shirt. With each passing second, my fingers longed to reach out and touch each muscle, indentation, and bulge.

If I could do as I pleased, had he?

Was I violated?

My gaze went over my arms and shoulders, down to my torso. A smile curled my lips at my inability to see any of my own skin besides my hands. I was still covered with the dressing gown. The clock beside the bed told me it was nearly three in the morning. I could wake him or curl against the warmth radiating beside me.

Before my decision was made, Roman's long lashes fluttered as his dark orbs focused on me. He sat up with a start. "You're awake."

"I am," I said as warmth filled my cheeks. "I'm sorry. I don't know what happened."

He was now sitting, his hair mussed and his long legs bent as he faced me—faced me without a shirt. "You fainted. Your complexion was ghostly white. I caught you before you hit the floor."

"I've never fainted before. I remember everything got wobbly."

Smiling, he took my hand. "I'm not much of a doctor, but I assessed you were breathing. I should have called Lady Buckingham." He took a deep breath. "I'm not confident on who to trust."

With the warmth of his touch covering my hands, I met his gaze. "I'm glad you didn't call for her. I think I trust you."

Roman's expression changed. "Do you think you were drugged?"

I hadn't.

I hadn't considered it.

My eyes opened wide. "I don't know what to believe any longer."

Roman hurried from the bed, going to the highboy and pouring water from the pitcher. Soon he was back with a glass of water. "Here, drink this. If you were drugged, this will help cleanse your system."

I took the cup and drank the cool water. Until I swallowed, I hadn't realized how thirsty I was. "May I have another?"

Taking the cup, he returned to the highboy and back to me. His dark stare glistened as he handed me the cup. "I was wrong not to get you help."

"No. I'm not sad we're alone."

His smile returned. "It's good to see you sitting up and hear your voice."

I patted the bed at my side.

Soon, Roman was back where he'd been sleeping except he was again sitting, facing me.

With my smile returning, I did what I'd wanted to do when I first laid eyes on his defined torso. I lifted my hand and splayed my fingers on his wide chest. The patch of dark hair was soft. The warmth within him radiated from him to me. Like electricity, the sensation tingled from the tips of my fingers and continued throughout my circulation. When I looked up, my smile had grown. "You are definitely not Roman."

"The reason for the padded shirt."

Untying the sash of my dressing gown, I pulled my arms from the long sleeves. As I did, Roman's gaze scanned from my eyes to my breasts.

"You are beautiful."

"Roman saw that as a fault."

"I don't. I see you for what you are, Lucille. Your looks are beyond stunning, but it's your sincerity and what you have inside you that is truly mesmerizing."

"We were to talk," I reminded him.

"That was hours ago."

"You should go back to your bedchamber."

His dark eyes shimmered. "Is that what you want me to do?"

I shook my head and reached toward him. As Roman's hand grasped mine, I felt a pull that had been absent for too long. When I looked up, my eyes were moist. Using the back of my other hand, I wiped away the tears before they could fall.

"Talk to me," Roman said. It was his voice, his face, yet again, the tone and timbre were wrong—and oh so right.

Inhaling, I feigned a smile. "I wish you were real."

He scooted closer, cupping my cheek. "I panicked when you collapsed. My first thought was that you'd been drugged, a safety net to prevent us from" —he tilted his head— "taking part in marital relations." Concern showed in his expression. "If that's the case, my presence is endangering you. I don't want that."

I could get lost in the way he looked at me. His penetrating gaze was as if what was once filled with ice was exploding, bursting with flames. A supernova consuming the space once occupied by a black hole.

Was that how it worked?

My thoughts were too irregular to concentrate.

"Why did you bring me back to my bedchamber?" I asked.

"I don't know," Roman said in an unfamiliar sincere tone. "I wanted you to wake where you felt safe and secure. I tucked you in and paced for hours. I shouldn't have lain beside you." He looked down at our hands and back to me. "I didn't want to leave you."

"You aren't endangering me. You're fulfilling your promise to be with me." I lifted my fist, covering a yawn. "Thank you."

"I should go."

Although he'd said the words, he didn't move.

"Or you could stay," I suggested. "I'm afraid to admit it, but I feel safe with you here."

His stunning smile lifted his cheeks and brought life to his gaze. "I'll stay and be gone before Lady Buckingham returns or Lord Martin arrives."

After turning off the lights, Roman turned back the covers on his side of the bed and unlike when I woke, he scooted underneath them. As he settled, I rolled toward him. "We don't do this."

His strong arm came around me, pulling me closer, providing his hard shoulder for my pillow. "Perhaps it is time we start."

"I wish it were that easy."

Roman kissed the top of my head. "Good night, my princess."

"Good night, my prince."

CHAPTER 28

Oliver

I turned to the windows within my office.

White.

The glaring white of millions of blinding crystals reflecting the sun's glow beneath a blue sky. The entire region of Monovia was covered by a thick blanket. While the accumulation had stopped growing, the wind continued whipping the snow about, creating drifts resembling waves on the sea.

The scene made me cold, yet memories of Lucille turned up the heat.

After I'd tucked her into her own bed, I spent hours pacing back and forth. Pacing had never been a thing for me until recently. Perhaps it was because my only space to fully be myself was within the confines of my bedchamber. Last night, I added Lucille's bedchamber to that list.

I should trust Lady Buckingham.

I should.

How many times had she seen bruises or marks left

by Roman and turned a blind eye? If the answer to that question was one, it was too many. Then again, who would Lady Buckingham go to on the chain of command.

The queen?
The king?

An incoming call rang from my computer.

Shielding my eyes, I sat and looked at the man—no, king—on the computer screen. "Your Grace," I said, addressing King Theodore.

"Lord Taylor tells me he's pleased with your understanding of what is expected at the coming summit."

"I've also been looking into the recent food shortages in the different regions."

He shook his head. "Don't overdo, son. You can't solve all of Molave's issues in a few weeks. This is a marathon, not a sprint."

I agreed; however, I had some thoughts. "If I may, sir, recently, there have been shipping problems near the ports in Molave. If instead of bringing the imports to Molave, the ships went north into Sognefjord, the grain could be brought directly to Monovia, Forthwith, and other smaller ports."

King Theodore leaned back and stared into the camera. "I like your initiative. Currently, the problems in the North Sea are our own doing. There's a plan in motion. Continue to work on the issues Lord Taylor instructs. Those are the matters you'll be expected to discuss."

"I was informed that deputies from the ministry have searched Annabella Castle."

"All within the jurisdiction of the royal guard. Standard."

It wasn't the royal guard but the deputies of the ministry.

"Were you aware?" I asked, uncertain if I believed.

"Of course I was aware. Nothing happens in Molave without my knowledge."

By the time our conversation neared the conclusion, I was equal parts annoyed and curious. It was as if I was to learn all there was to know about one subject while being willfully blind on others.

"Tell me about Princess Lucille," the king prompted.

"We don't speak," I said, fully aware of my blatant lie.

King Theodore nodded. "Our desire is for her health." His dark eyes narrowed. "She hasn't been ill, has she?"

"No, Your Grace, not to my knowledge. I will inquire."

He shook his head with a smile. "No need, son.

We'll get those roads cleared. The princess has an appointment in nine days."

Sealing my lips and nodding was the extent of my reply. Thankfully, the subject moved on to other issues of state. It wasn't until evening that I even laid eyes on the princess. Returning to our private apartment, I stopped in the connecting parlor, hearing voices from Lucille's side.

With the doors slightly ajar, I couldn't stop my curiosity.

Through the small opening, I saw Lucille's profile and the back of Lady Buckingham's head. It was an unusual opportunity to watch the princess without her knowledge. Silently, I stared as the two women competed in a game of chess. The way Lucille concentrated and her smile bloomed with pride stirred a feeling inside me I hadn't had in—ever.

"Your Highness."

I spun toward the sound of my address and the opening of the door. Clearing my throat, I stepped away from Lucille's doors. "Lord Martin."

"She is beautiful."

My eyebrows lowered. "She's the princess. Her beauty isn't for you or anyone to discuss."

"They do. The people, the papers, and social media—they all discuss it at length."

"She is an asset to this country, and she's kept locked away on a mountaintop."

Lord Martin nodded. "It is complicated. Perhaps if the procedure is a success..."

"And if it isn't, I'm to discard her."

Lord Martin opened the door to my suite and bowed. "I'll help you ready for dinner."

Once the door was closed, I turned. "She's given this country over five years and the king wants to throw her away?"

"No, Your Highness. The duchess will be compensated. The people will never allow the divorce to be private. It will demonstrate the generosity of the crown despite her failure as princess."

"She hasn't failed..." I sucked in a breath. "Have you heard any additional information regarding Borinkia's princess?"

"No. Annabella is rather isolated. Once we return to Molave City, I will keep my eyes and ears open. If I hear anything, Your Highness, I will inform you."

Two hours later, Lucille and I were seated in our connecting parlor, our dinner in front of us. It was nearly impossible not to stare or notice the way she would veil her light blue gaze beneath her lush lashes.

The princess was stunning in a dark blue knit dress that hugged her soft curves yet covered the delicate skin I'd seen last night. Throughout our dinner, I had so many things I wanted to say to Lucille.

"I will not call for you tonight," I said as we finished our meal.

Lucille's expression saddened. "Your Highness."

I lowered my voice. "Summoning you could end up with the same result as last night. Tonight, come to me without a summons."

"I do not," she said.

"Tonight, you will."

Pink filled her cheeks as she nodded. "Yes, Your Highness."

Later that night, I paced my bedchamber, wondering if Lucille would do as I said and come to me of her own accord. As the time on the clock was almost ten, I debated. I could go to her side and behave as Roman, admonishing her for not doing as she was told, or I could be a gentleman and leave her to her own choices.

What if she'd been drugged again?

The new fear prickled my skin and fueled my determination.

As I flung open the door to the bedchamber and stalked toward the doors to the connecting parlor, I told myself it was about Lucille's safety. That was all.

Opening the door to the parlor, I sucked in a breath, coming face-to-face with Princess Lucille.

"Your Highness," she said with a curtsy.

I didn't say a word as I stepped back and bid her entry. It wasn't until the door was closed that I cupped her cheeks and brought her lips to mine. "I was worried."

Her blue orbs swirled with darker hues. "That I wouldn't come?"

"That we were overheard, and you were lying on the floor drugged."

Her smile warmed me from within. "I'm enjoying the clandestine encounters. There's a spontaneity we lacked."

"I wish this were a game, Lucille. I would play it with you every night." My timbre slowed. "It isn't a game. I'm fearful for you."

"Don't be, Roman. I've been here for long enough to understand the rules. I just want to be here...with you." She looked around. "You called me here. What do you want to do now?"

"What I shouldn't," I said, my tone and timbre dropping as I led her back to my bedchamber.

Once inside with the door closed, Lucille reached for my hand, lifting, turning, and studying it. "That's Roman's wedding ring."

"Or a good imitation."

"Take it off," she demanded. Almost instantaneously, she looked up and her tone mellowed. "Your

Highness, not because I don't want you to wear it. I want to see the inside. Very few people know of the inscription."

Twisting the diamond-encrusted gold band, I pulled the ring from my finger. Squinting at the writing inside, I read, "Happily ever after."

Lucille's chin dropped to her chest. "It's his. What has become of him?"

"I don't know," I answered honestly as I placed the band back on my fourth finger. "Happily ever after?"

"When we courted and when you proposed, you promised me a real-life fairy tale. Those made-up stories always end with that same sentence. I had it engraved after the ring was fitted for you."

I reached for her hand. "I'm sorry he didn't make it come true."

"He changed. I can't explain it. His social anxiety got worse and with it his quickness to anger. Isabella said he was jealous."

"Maybe we can make it work," I said. It was a crazy thing to say. A husband wasn't replaceable with a look-alike, and yet I'd given a vow. I'd make one to Lucille too.

She shook her head. "I'm afraid—afraid of the consequences. The reality hit me again yesterday when I dared to lash out. It isn't something I would do, not before."

"You had every right, Lucille. I never should have taken the risk." I squeezed her hand. "Multi-tasking. I was working with Lord Taylor and thinking about being alone with you. Since last night, it's all I want to think about."

"We're alone."

CHAPTER
29

Oliver

"Princess." My voice was gravelly with pent-up desire. "I want you more than I should."

"I want you, too."

"Your vow," I reminded. Though my body wanted me to leave the real Roman out of this equation, I'd become too infatuated with this woman to take advantage of her position. I'd even used the word love when speaking to the senator. It wasn't rehearsed. It just slipped out.

Exhaling, Lucille pulled back the blankets on the bed and untied the sash of her dressing gown. With her blue gaze transfixed on me, she pushed the dressing gown from her shoulders, allowing it to fall to the carpet.

As she stood, I scanned from her flowing long hair to her mesmerizing stare, her kissable lips, and lower. Lace straps over her shoulders kept her long white satin nightgown in place. She was an angel sent to earth.

I was the impostor who didn't deserve her.

Lucille's breasts pushed forward with each breath as she stared at me. "I've forgotten what it was like to be desired. Even without words, I feel desired by you."

Pulling the pajama top with the Godfrey crest over my head, I stood before her in only satin pajama bottoms. Lucille would have to be blind to not see my desire tenting the pants.

"You are desired, Lucille." I reached for her hands, holding them between us, as she craned her neck upward to maintain our eye contact. "Roman was a fool if he didn't desire you."

"He did and then he didn't."

"I won't be your reason for eternal damnation that comes with breaking your vow."

"I've been damned, Roman. The last five years have been hell on earth. I don't know if Roman kept his vow to me. I suspected he didn't, but I was never brave enough to ask."

Cupping her cheek in my palm, I sensed the warmth of her skin as she inclined her face to my touch. "I've never been married."

"Are you telling me that you're a virgin?"

The chuckle bubbled from my throat. "No, that isn't what I'm saying. I've never broken a commitment, a vow, or cheated in a relationship. I've broken off relationships and been cheated on by others, but my word is true."

"Such a kingly thing to say."

"I'm no king," I replied. "However, I did make a vow to Molave, and if I am going to keep it, I want it all. I want you at my side."

Fuck the idea of a divorce.

Taking my hand in hers, Lucille led it to her shoulder, prompting me to push the lace down her arm. I didn't need her assistance with the other strap. My mouth went dry, and the temperature of the room rose exponentially as her nightgown fluttered to the floor. With a white puddle of satin around her feet, the princess stood before me the way God had made her, beautifully nude.

Unable to stop myself, I reached out, running my touch over her flesh and down her arms as my gaze scanned her pert breasts, flat stomach, shaved mound, slightly rounded hips and ass, and then lower to her shapely legs.

"To say you're beautiful is doing you an injustice, Princess."

Her blue eyes sparkled. "Last night, I wore bloomers. Tonight..." As she spoke, her smile grew. "I hoped if I didn't have them, you would remove the pajama pants?"

"If that's what you want."

"I do."

If this were a movie instead of real life, there would be intensifying music. The camera would focus on our expressions and take close-ups of where we touched one another. It wasn't only I who sought the connection. Lucille's fingertips left a ghostly touch over my shoulders, abdomen, and back. It was as she reached out and ran her hand up and down my penis that lights flashed and rockets launched.

If she continued, I'd be done for the night or at least for a while. Seizing her hand, I brought it to my lips. Seeing the glint in her eyes, I grinned. "I expected you to be timid."

"I usually am."

"I'm usually not."

Lucille took a step closer, pressing her body against mine and pinning my erection against her stomach. "Don't be."

"You don't know what you're asking."

She pushed up on her tiptoes, bringing her lips to mine. Her hands held tight to my shoulders as our kiss deepened. Step by step, I moved us until her shoulders collided with the bookcase. When she looked up, her lips were pink from our kiss and her blue stare was veiled. "I'm asking you to remind me what it's like to have someone truly desire me."

Lifting her ass, I sandwiched her between me and

the bookcase, hoping to God that at its age, it would hold up to what I had in mind. Her heels came to my lower back as she wrapped her legs around me.

After all I'd been through—all we'd both been through—having Lucille in my grasp was a fantasy come to life. The bedchamber filled with her mews and moans as we went between kisses and nips. Lucille gave as much as she took. My teeth teased her soft skin as her lips peppered my neck and shoulders.

As I lowered my attention, there were no blankets to obscure her round tits. Her back arched as I sucked one nipple and then the other.

Balancing her petite frame with my arm, I teased her folds.

"I want—"

She placed a finger on my lips. "Don't ask. The answer is yes. You aren't taking. I'm giving."

"Fuck," I growled as two fingers slid into her wet core.

Lucille's body trembled as she bounced with my rhythm. The grip on my shoulders intensified as with my thumb, I swirled her clit. Her heels dug into my lower back as she gasped, and her core convulsed around my fingers. I didn't stop until Lucille went slack, collapsing against my shoulder.

"That was..." she lifted her face, as her radiant smile grew. "I haven't done that in a long time."

"Well, Princess, if you're up to more, so am I."

"I noticed," she said with a sensational grin. Before I could respond, she again placed her finger over my lips. "I'm here, Roman. If I didn't want whatever you're up for, I would be across the apartments in my own bedchamber."

Seizing her hips, I lifted her, cradling her against my chest as I carried her back to the bed. Lucille bounced with a giggle as I followed a step behind. Her long hair flowed over her shoulders as she scooted toward the headboard.

I crawled over her, my gaze meeting hers.

No longer was Lucille untouchable, a royal, or Molave's princess. In this bedchamber, with her hair tousled and blotches of pink on her skin, she was simply breathtaking, stunning, and captivating. It was as if for a moment in time she had given herself the freedom to step beyond those boundaries—freedom to be herself.

Lifting her knees to either side of me, Lucille offered what was only hers to give. It was a gift I couldn't repay, yet as I lined up my hardened cock, I had an overpowering need to be honest.

"Look at me." My accent was gone.

Her crystal-clear blue stare was millimeters before me.

"My name is Oliver."

"Mine is Lucille."

"Tell me to stop. I can't promise I will, but this is your last chance."

Her petite palms framed my cheeks. "Don't stop, Oliver. Never stop. The only way this will work is if we are in it together."

My eyes closed and a roar came from my lips as I brought us together. Buried to the root we were completely and utterly united as one.

As her pussy squeezed with the intensity of a vise grip, I was too lost in the moment. Her noises of pleasure, the way she writhed beneath me, and her receptiveness to each and every touch had me on sensory overload.

More than once, Lucille came undone before I reached my precipice. The fall from the cliff was climactic and earthquaking. When I finally fell slack over her soft frame, Lucille's arms wrapped around me, holding me to her.

Lifting my head, I met her stare. "I hope you aren't regretting your decision."

Her lips quirked. "I only regret that you aren't real."

"I'm real, Princess."

"No matter what happens, I want you to know, Oliver, you were sent to me by the heavens. In this short time, you've given me more than I can say."

Closing my eyes, I moved, breaking our union. As I rolled to my back, Lucille followed.

With her hands on my chest, she lifted her eyes to mine. "I'm glad to know your name."

"Never use it again."

"Only in my heart, Your Highness."

I didn't think to tell her that I'd been cleared by Mr. Davies, that despite my last relationship, I was disease free. That thought didn't come until later when we were basking in the afterglow.

CHAPTER
30

Lucille

"Your Highness," I said, standing with a curtsy in our shared parlor as Roman entered from his suite. Resuming my seat, I gestured across the table. "Your breakfast arrived."

This was our fourth morning to meet over breakfast after spending a part of the night together. While the first night he summoned me did not result in a sexual encounter, our desire for one another grew with each passing day. The night after I secretly went to him, Roman came to me. With most of the castle quiet, he snuck into my suite. I'd first heard the click of the outer doors before the door to my bedchamber opened.

"I tried to stay away."

The memory of his confession brought a smile to my face.

Last night, I'd been the one to cross the parlor. He hadn't summoned me, but that didn't stop me. Once I was certain Lord Martin was gone, I did as he'd done and opened doors without a knock. It was a comfort level I'd only dreamed of obtaining, with anyone.

In reality, we'd only known of one another for little over a month. However, our reality was skewed—a reflection of what was to be seen. In that reflection we were beyond our fifth wedding anniversary. And yet we'd shared more, spoken more, and touched more freely in the last four days. My thoughts went to last night.

The exertion of our encounter could be heard in our rapid breaths and seen in the shimmer of perspiration upon our skin. Roman's palm cupped my cheek. "I don't want you to go back to your bedchamber."

His dark eyes swirled with the intensity of his desire. I found myself lost in the changing hues. His laser-sharp focus was like a drug circulating through my blood stream. The high it instilled coursed throughout every fiber of my being, bringing synapse after synapse to life—a series of explosions. The more I had, the more I wanted.

As Roman severed our connection, I craned my neck and lifted my bruised lips to his. "I don't want to go. This, whatever it is" —I took a breath— "my heart wants to confess my love and devotion." Before Roman could speak, I recognized the absurdity of my comment. With my eyes veiled, I added, "You don't need to say anything. I know this isn't real. I just wish..."

Roman lifted my chin until our eyes met. "I love you, Lucille. I'm losing touch with what is real and what's not." His smile grew as he rolled onto his back and lifted me over him. As his strong hands held tight to my hips, he said, "You feel real."

With my hands on his wide shoulders, I sat upward, my long hair cascading down, a veil separating us from the world, as Roman's erection prodded against my behind. The man beneath me took my breath away. It wasn't simply his beautiful, almost movie-star appearance. It was more. Unlike the man before him, this man's handsomeness wasn't purely his looks. With him, it was deeper: his heart, his devotion, and his honesty. It was in the way he listened, spoke, and touched. "I'm real," I confessed. "If it were within my means, I'd make this real."

Teasing long locks of my hair over my shoulders, Roman's gaze skirted my face and down to my breasts. With the concentration of his stare, my pulse sped and my breathing shallowed.

"Don't leave, not yet," he commanded.

Before I could reply, Roman lifted my hips and aligned me to reconnect as one.

My body tensed. "You don't allow this."

"This?"

"Me on top." My cheeks warmed. "You are always in control."

"*Princess, there's no threat in sharing control. It's the only way a true partnership will work. Having you beneath me is heaven. Being beneath you is like watching the creation of a masterpiece. Control is yours too if only you'll take it.*"

I contemplated the opportunity before me. Slowly, I lifted myself on my bent knees. Scooting back until his erection was before me, I fisted his penis, slick from our earlier lovemaking, and aligned him to me. An addicting concoction of anticipation and power brought my senses to life as I closed my eyes and took the control he offered. My nipples grew taut as I sheathed Roman with my core. When I opened my eyes, I was met with the handsomest smile I'd ever seen.

"*You're stunning, Lucille.*"

Moving up and down, I marveled at the sense of fullness as well as the ability to set the pace. A few more ups and downs, and I smiled as my cheeks grew warmer. "I think I like this."

"*You'd better be sure. Because watching your changing expressions is magnificent. I'd promise the entirety of my life to Molave to see that display nightly.*"

That was last night.

During the day, we'd both become adept at hiding our true feeling behind the masks of our roles. However, the prince's expression from last night was no longer present.

I looked up to Roman's soured countenance. "Your Highness," I said, "are you troubled?"

His dark gaze went from side to side.

"We are alone."

We'd both searched high and low for cameras or listening devices. As in the palace in Molave City, the private apartments seemed clean. It made no sense that the king or the Firm would need to overhear our private thoughts.

I nodded.

"The roads are cleared," he said. "I'm expected back in Molave City."

The sadness in his expression settled over me with the reality that soon I'd be left alone, again. "I understand."

Roman reached across the table and covered my hand with his. "I want you to come with me."

"You wouldn't."

He stood, throwing his napkin onto his chair. "I'm the prince."

In his rare bursts of anger and with his padded shirt beneath his suit, it was difficult to distinguish that this was Oliver instead of Roman. Part of me wished I didn't know his real name. The other part of me was honored that he'd shared something with me that not even Lord Martin knew.

"Yes, Your Highness."

Roman stopped, crouching down at my side. "I'll make you a promise. I'll do whatever I need to do to get us back together. Either you to Molave City or me here."

The overpowering sadness at the mention of his departure stole my words, leaving me to simply nod.

"I hate that you're lonely."

"I have my memories of you. That's more than I've had in the past. And in less than a week, I'll be due for my procedure. I would suspect I'll be called to Molave City for that."

"Fucking ridiculous," Roman murmured as he stood and walked back to his chair.

"You could express your concerns to King Theo."

Roman smirked. "If I were truly Roman, perhaps. You are to be off-limits until the procedure is deemed a success."

Until?

I gasped as I stared at the man lifting a cup of tea to his lips. "Did the king say that?"

Roman nodded.

Standing, I walked to the fireplace and looked at my own reflection in the large mirror. "It's as if I'm the one not real." I spun. "The king would allow you, a man other than the one I married, to bed me as if my body was his to grant?"

"Shh," Roman scolded, speaking low. "Remember, you, Princess, don't raise your voice."

"I should."

"Yes, you should, but you don't." His smile quirked. "Are you angry that the king would grant what you've already allowed?"

"Yes." I stood tall. "It isn't his to give. I'm not his to give. I'm no one's to give."

Again, dropping his napkin to the seat of his chair, Roman stalked my way. His posture and attempt at a riled expression would have sent chills through me a month ago. Now I saw the gleam in his dark orbs. Reaching for my shoulders, he looked into my gaze and nodded. "Thank you."

I exhaled. "It was my choice. I decided."

"You did." His lips came to my forehead.

Looking up, I added, "It's not right that he would dare..."

"It's not. Know, Lucille, the king making it so would not have made me take it from you."

I lifted my chin. "I'm glad we went against the king and the physician."

Roman smiled, leaving another kiss on my forehead. "If I could commission a plane to announce to the world that you're mine, I would. You are after all my wife." His eyes grew larger. "That's it."

"Skywriting or a banner? I'm not certain those are the answer to anything."

"The tour of North America."

"Not until the new year," I reminded him.

"Right." His head was nodding as he paced back and forth. "That gives me some more time with the king. I will try to lengthen the tour, maybe include other countries."

"Whatever for? Tours are dreadful."

"No, don't you see?" Before I could respond, Roman went on. "It will be our chance. The people of Molave love you, Lucille. The entire world is infatuated with you. While we have those eyes upon us, we will be able to break down the barrier between us. Once our affection is on public display, the king will have no say."

"Until Roman returns." Even saying the words left a sour taste in my mouth.

"And then you leave him."

"My father offered his help," I said, walking back to my toast and jam.

Roman gripped my arm, spinning me back. "Say that again."

My gaze went to his hold and back. "What is the matter? You're hurting me."

With a shake of his head, Roman released my arm. "Lucille, what did you say about your father?"

"When he was in Molave City to meet with you, he asked if I was well. He said if I called, he'd arrange for the US Embassy to assist with getting me back to America."

"Why?" Roman asked. "I thought you didn't tell them you were unhappy."

"I haven't." I shrugged. "You saw my displeasure when I didn't even know you. They are my parents."

"What did you say?"

"That I didn't want a divorce."

Now seated across from me, Roman leaned forward and in a hushed tone asked, "What do you know of the princess of Borinkia?"

"Nothing."

It was all I could say before there was a knock on the door and Lord Martin and Lady Buckingham entered. Of course, they'd both been present earlier, waking each of us and dressing each of us. After our breakfast was delivered, they went their own way. Now with a bow and a curtsy, they were back.

"I'll put your schedule in your parlor," Lady Buckingham said to me.

Lord Martin made a similar comment before they both disappeared into our respective suites.

"Can you tell me more?" I whispered.

Roman mouthed his response silently. "Later." His dark eyes looked toward his bedchamber and back to me. "Lord Taylor will travel today. I'm tired of his presence." He sat taller, his voice louder. "I have decided that I will postpone my return to Molave City until tomorrow."

"Your Highness?" Lord Martin asked as he appeared through the double doors. "The king is expecting you."

Roman stood, his neck straightening as he turned toward his assistant. "Lord Martin, as crown prince I am at no one's beck and call. The king will need to wait."

Lord Martin's eyes opened wide as he stared from Roman to me and back to Roman.

"Leave us," Roman proclaimed.

"Sir, Lord Taylor is waiting in your office suite."

"Once I finish my meal, I'll be down."

Lord Martin nodded as Lady Buckingham entered from my suite.

"Leave us," he said again.

The hostility of his tone faded with the closing of the door. It was impossible to contain my grin. "You're truly improving."

His smile was back with a quirk and a gleam in his brown eyes. "We will talk. The sooner I meet with Lord Taylor, the sooner he will leave. Tonight, we will dine."

"Yes, Your Highness."

CHAPTER
31

Lucille

Our evening meal was complete, the dishes taken away. While the sun had finally shown during the day, the skies were now black and speckled with a peppering of stars. It was too early in the year for the frigid temperatures that followed the snow, yet they were here. The melt had not come as they anticipated, locking us inside the castle.

As Lady Buckingham brushed my hair, I thought about how lonely it would be once Roman was gone.

The door to the bedchamber opened with a slam as Lady Buckingham and I turned to the sight of Roman standing in the doorway between the bathroom and bedchamber, still dressed in his suit pants and his wrinkled white shirt. His tie and jacket from dinner were gone. Gripping the doorjamb, he looked from me to my mistress.

"You're dismissed for the night," he said, addressing Lady Buckingham.

"Your Highness," she said with a curtsy, placing the hairbrush on my dressing table. Her gaze came to mine, questioning while placating. That was what she did even when she knew my night was to turn unbearable. I saw it now.

Lady Buckingham nodded with a quizzical glance toward the prince and obeying his order, exited my suite.

"Have you been drinking?" I asked softly.

"Yes." Roman's voice was too loud. "As a matter of fact, I have. I recommend it."

"Roman," I cautioned, walking toward him. Each step took me deeper into a cloud of cologne and bourbon. "Don't ruin things."

His large palms framed my cheeks as he pulled my lips to his. There was no hesitation as his tongue sought entrance. It was too much too fast. My fingers balled to fists as I pounded against his chest, my hits bouncing off the added padding.

"Stop," I screamed when I broke free. Wrapping my arms around myself with my eyes opened too wide and unwanted fear coursing through my circulation, I backed away. "What are you doing?"

Roman ran his hand over his dark hair. "Acting, remember." He lifted his finger to his lips and walked toward the connecting parlor. When he returned, he reached for my hand and fell to one knee. "I'm sorry, Princess. I couldn't wait another hour."

The sight of him genuflecting brought a smile to my lips. "Roman, I don't understand."

He stood with a kiss to my cheek. "Something has been bothering me."

"Only one thing?"

He tugged on my hand. "Look at your bedchamber."

I turned a full circle. "I've lived here for five years. What do you want me to see?"

"Come with me."

Without a word, Roman led me from my bedchamber, out my suite, across the parlor, and through the double doors into his suite. "Think about your bedchamber."

I nodded as we stepped into his.

"Why is it different?" he asked. "Everything else is the same, only reversed."

"It isn't different," I said, turning another circle.

"It is." Roman walked to the bookcases and began stepping heel to toe across the room. His dark gaze met mine. "Twenty-seven."

I followed as he hurried back to my side.

Starting at my bookcases, he paced, heel to toe. "Thirty-three."

"I don't know," I admitted. "My side is bigger. I'm female. I have more clothes."

"But don't you see, it isn't the closet. It's the entire side of the room. This has been gnawing at me since the night you were drugged. I'd spent much of that night pacing in your bedchamber. Before I came to Annabella, I studied the blueprints. There was no indication that the suites were different in any way."

"Right after we married, you—Roman—insisted on renovations. Prior to us taking residence, Annabella Castle had been used only as a vacation home." I shrugged. "While I wasn't consulted about the renovations, I appreciated the upgrades, especially to our bathrooms."

Roman's forehead furrowed. "After you were married?"

I nodded. "I'm sure if you spoke to King Theo—"

Roman's eyes opened wide as he hurried back to his bedchamber.

I followed a step behind, shaking my head. "This game of tag wasn't how I imagined spending our last night together."

"Bear with me." Roman walked along the bookshelves. "You may think I'm mad."

"Or it's the liquor."

His smile grew as he peered at me sideways. "I didn't drink, not much. It was for effect."

A scoff came from my throat. "You had me fooled."

"And you, Princess, are my most important audience." He continued running his hands under each shelf.

"What are you looking for?"

"All the movies have them." His gaze met mine. "A secret passage."

Crossing my arms over my breasts, I leaned against the wall. "I told you, Americans think they know royal life. They don't. You still don't. Everything is a reflection of reality."

"Fuck," Roman mumbled as he stepped back. As we stood in silence, the second bookcase on the left moved backward.

My lips opened in surprise as it then swung to the left. My heart rate sped as Roman's wide eyes met mine. "Shit," I said, walking to his side and reaching for his arm.

"This is what the deputies of the ministry have been searching for," he said.

"Should we call them?"

Roman shook his head. "No, Princess. If we're in this together as we've agreed, my gut is telling me that we need whatever is inside that room."

My grip of his arm intensified. "I'm frightened."

His handsome smile shone down on me as he moved my hand from his arm to his grasp. "I can't promise you won't be afraid, Lucille. I can only promise that as long as I'm here, you won't be alone. I'll be here with you."

Swallowing, I nodded.

"Wait." Roman went to his bedside stand and unplugged his cellphone. Soon, it was a flashlight, shining a bright beam. With that in one hand, and his other hand holding mine, we went forward, into the darkness. The floor was colder within the hidden room as dust floated in the beam of the light.

Roman directed the flashlight along each wall. The far end contained another bookcase filled to overflowing. Along the walls were stacks of totes. I ran my finger over the top of one, creating a line in the dust.

"It's not very big." I said, my voice echoing.

"It's the full length of the room, but you're right" — he shrugged— "no more than five feet wide."

"One and a half meters," I corrected.

"Yeah, it's shit like that I forget," Roman said with a grin. "Help me find a light."

I ran my hands over the wall on one side as Roman did the same on the other. "I found a switch," I called out, pushing it upward.

We both squinted at the onslaught of illumination.

"There's no reason for this space," I said, walking toward the far end. "There's plenty of room in your office for books."

"Roman didn't want this found."

"Then why have it? My mother warned against recording anything that could be used against you."

Roman lifted the first book on the left from the top shelf and opened it to the first page. "Shit, it's a journal." His dark gaze zeroed in on me. "When were you married?"

"July seventeenth."

He read the year.

Nodding, I wrapped my arms around my midsection as my hands began to tremble. "What date is that?"

"September third of the same year."

"We were back from our honeymoon and had moved into here." I stepped closer. "What does it say?"

CHAPTER 32

Oliver

My eyes widened as I took in the words. I could have written the entry before me. The handwriting was familiar. That wasn't what could have made it mine. It was the words. This seemed impossible to comprehend, but as I scanned the page, my gut told me it wasn't impossible. After all, the Firm had found me.

Lucille reached for my arm, her touch cold and trembling.

"Come," I said, "let's take this out into the bedchamber."

"Roman, what does it say?"

I didn't want to tell Lucille what I'd read. Seeing the worry in her blue eyes, I wanted the opposite, to make her happy. However, she'd been the one to say we were in this together. Maybe if Roman, the last Roman, had trusted her, things would have ended differently.

The temperature rose as we returned to the

bedchamber. I led Lucille to the bed. "Here," I said, lifting back the blankets. "You're shivering." I saw her bare feet beneath the hem of the nightgown.

It seemed that during each monumental juncture in our short relationship, Lucille was without shoes.

Doing as I said, Princess Lucille scooted under the covers and continued moving, making room for me. Her blue eyes pleaded, giving impact to her words. "Please, sit with me. Whatever this is, I don't want to learn it alone."

I nodded as I kicked off my loafers and slid under the covers still wearing my shirt and pants. Opening the journal, I began reading the handwritten entry.

"If anyone is reading this, I've failed and been replaced."

The words hit me with the impact of a physical punch. I turned to Lucille, wondering what she could possibly be thinking.

"Go on," she said.

"Are you sure?"

She nodded.

I continued reading. "I haven't decided to chronicle my life to earn your sympathy at my passing. I don't deserve that. I took this assignment. I agreed to take the vow to move from being no one to being someone, to becoming royalty, as if that's even possible. I'm new and still learning.

What I didn't realize until it was too late is that ruling Molave is a ruthless task, and King Theodore will continue his ruthless reign no matter who is at his side.

"My real name was Noah Evans. A few days ago and until my last breath, my name is Roman Archibald Godfrey. I signed that name and took the place of the crown prince as the heir apparent to the throne of Molave and at the side of Roman's new bride, Lucille Sutton. She isn't to know that I'm not the man she married..."

"Oh my God," Lucille cried, her face falling to her hands. "How is this possible?"

My mind too was scrambling. "There's an entire shelf of journals. Probably a hundred."

Tears flowed from the princess's eyes. "Why? How? Nothing has been real."

Clenching my jaw, I wrapped my arm around Lucille, pulling her quaking body to mine, and vowed to learn the truth. There was one man with the answers, that same man who had replaced his son more than once.

I wasn't sure how, but I'd stay resilient in my new vow. Theodore Godfrey's ruthless reign would end on my watch.

* * *

I hope you've enjoyed RUTHLESS REIGN and will come back for more in RESILIENT REIGN coming January 2023. Oliver and Lucille's story isn't complete. There is much more of Royal Reflections coming. Tell your friends to start this series today with RUTHLESS REIGN.

What to do now

LEND IT: Did you enjoy RUTHLESS REIGN? Do you have a friend who'd enjoy RUTHLESS REIGN? RUTHLESS REIGN may be lent one time. Sharing is caring!

RECOMMEND IT: Do you have multiple friends who'd enjoy my dark romance with twists and turns and an all new sexy and infuriating anti-hero? Tell them about it! Call, text, post, tweet...your recommendation is the nicest gift you can give to an author!

REVIEW IT: Tell the world. Please go to the retailer where you purchased this book, as well as Goodreads, and write a review. Please share your thoughts about RUTHLESS REIGN on:

*Amazon, RUTHLESS REIGN Customer Reviews

*Barnes & Noble, RUTHLESS REIGN, Customer Reviews

*Apple Books, RUTHLESS REIGN Customer Reviews

* BookBub, RUTHLESS REIGN Customer Reviews

*Goodreads.com/Aleatha Romig

Books by ALEATHA

ROYAL REFLECTIONS SERIES:

RILED REIGN (prequel)

September 2022

RUTHLESS REIGN

November 2022

RESILIENT REIGN

January 2023

READY TO BINGE:

SIN SERIES:

Prequel: WHITE RIBBON

August 2021

RED SIN

October 2021

GREEN ENVY

January 2022

GOLD LUST

April 2022

BLACK KNIGHT

June 2022

STAND-ALONE ROMANTIC SUSPENSE:

KINGDOM COME

November 2021

DEVIL'S SERIES (Duet):

Prequel: "FATES DEMAND"

Prequel - March 18

DEVIL'S DEAL

May 2021

ANGEL'S PROMISE

June 2021

WEB OF SIN:

SECRETS

October 2018

LIES

December 2018

PROMISES

January 2019

TANGLED WEB:

TWISTED

May 2019

OBSESSED

July 2019

BOUND

August 2019

WEB OF DESIRE:

SPARK

Jan. 14, 2020

FLAME

February 25, 2020

ASHES

April 7, 2020

DANGEROUS WEB:

Prequel: "Danger's First Kiss"

DUSK

November 2020

DARK

January 2021

DAWN

February 2021

* * *

THE INFIDELITY SERIES:

BETRAYAL

Book #1

October 2015

CUNNING

Book #2

January 2016

DECEPTION

Book #3

May 2016

ENTRAPMENT

Book #4

September 2016

FIDELITY

Book #5

January 2017

* * *

THE CONSEQUENCES SERIES:

CONSEQUENCES

(Book #1)

August 2011

TRUTH

(Book #2)

October 2012

CONVICTED

(Book #3)

October 2013

REVEALED

(Book #4)

Previously titled: Behind His Eyes Convicted: The Missing Years

June 2014

BEYOND THE CONSEQUENCES

(Book #5)

January 2015

RIPPLES (Consequences stand-alone)

October 2017

CONSEQUENCES COMPANION READS:

BEHIND HIS EYES-CONSEQUENCES

January 2014

BEHIND HIS EYES-TRUTH

March 2014

* * *

STAND ALONE MAFIA THRILLER:

PRICE OF HONOR

Available Now

* * *

STAND-ALONE ROMANTIC THRILLER:

ON THE EDGE

May 2022

***

THE LIGHT DUET:

Published through Thomas and Mercer Amazon exclusive

INTO THE LIGHT

June 2016

AWAY FROM THE DARK

October 2016

* * *

TALES FROM THE DARK SIDE SERIES:

INSIDIOUS

(All books in this series are stand-alone erotic thrillers)

Released October 2014

* * *

ALEATHA'S LIGHTER ONES:

PLUS ONE

Stand-alone fun, sexy romance

May 2017

ANOTHER ONE

Stand-alone fun, sexy romance

May 2018

ONE NIGHT

Stand-alone, sexy contemporary romance

September 2017

A SECRET ONE

April 2018

MY ALWAYS ONE

Stand-one, sexy friends to lovers contemporary romance

July 2021

QUINTESSENTIALLY

Stand-alone, small-town, second-chance, secret baby
contemporary romance

July 2022

* * *

INDULGENCE SERIES:

UNEXPECTED

August 2018

UNCONVENTIONAL

January 2018

UNFORGETTABLE

October 2019

UNDENIABLE

August 2020

ABOUT THE AUTHOR

Aleatha Romig is a New York Times, Wall Street Journal, and USA Today bestselling author who lives in Indiana, USA. She has raised three children with her high school sweetheart and husband of over thirty years. Before she became a full-time author, she worked days as a dental hygienist and spent her nights writing. Now, when she's not imagining mind-blowing twists and turns, she likes to spend her time with her family and friends. Her other pastimes include reading and creating heroes/anti-heroes who haunt your dreams!

Aleatha impresses with her versatility in writing. She released her first novel, CONSEQUENCES, in August of 2011. CONSEQUENCES, a dark romance, became a bestselling series with five novels and two companions released from 2011 through 2015. The compelling and epic story of Anthony and Claire Rawlings has graced more than half a million e-readers. Her first stand-alone smart, sexy thriller INSIDIOUS was next. Then Aleatha released the five-novel INFIDELITY series, a romantic suspense saga, that took the reading world by storm, the final book landing on three of the top bestseller lists. She ventured into traditional publishing with Thomas and Mercer. Her books INTO THE LIGHT and AWAY FROM THE DARK were published through this mystery/thriller publisher in 2016.

In the spring of 2017, Aleatha again ventured into a different genre with her first fun and sexy stand-alone romantic comedy with the USA Today bestseller PLUS ONE. She continued the "Ones" series with additional standalones, ONE NIGHT, ANOTHER ONE, MY ALWAYS ONE, and QUINTESSEN-TIALLY THE ONE. If you like fun, sexy, novellas that make your heart pound, try her "Indulgence series" with UNCONVENTIONAL. UNEX-PECTED, UNFORGETTABLE, and UNDENIABLE.

In 2018 Aleatha returned to her dark romance roots with SPARROW WEBS. And continued with the mafia romance DEVIL'S DUET, and most recently her SIN series.

You may find all Aleatha's titles on her website.

Aleatha is a "Published Author's Network" member of the Romance Writers of America and PEN America. She is represented by Kevan Lyon of Marsal Lyon Literary Agency and Dani Sanchez with Wildfire Marketing.

facebook.com/aleatharomig

twitter.com/aleatharomig

instagram.com/aleatharomig

CPSIA information can be obtained
at www.ICGtesting.com
Printed in the USA
BVHW030706181022
649631BV00007B/9